Lee on the Dark Side of the Moon

Keith Charters

STRIDENT

Published by
Strident Publishing Ltd
22 Strathwhillan Drive
East Kilbride
G75 8GT

Tel: +44 (0)1355 220588
info@stridentpublishing.co.uk
www.stridentpublishing.co.uk

JF

© Keith Charters 2010

....

A catalogue record for this book is
available from the British Library.
ISBN 978-1-905537-13-6

Typeset in Gotham
Interior designed by Melvin Creative
Cover by Lawrence Mann
Printed by JF Print

Keith Charters

has lived all over the UK, and now lives near Glasgow.

He studied at the University of Strathclyde and should have gained a first class honours degree, but missed out by half a percent, mainly because he was playing snooker when he should have been studying. (Let this be a lesson to all.)

After graduating, Keith worked in various business management roles, ending up in London, where he headed up part of a big, rather strange, financial company in which staff got paid for shouting at their customers ... and at each other. It was weird.

At this point Keith started writing a lot. An awful lot. Soon writing was taking over his life. So he took a deep breath, gave up his 'proper' job and began writing full-time.

Lee and the Consul Mutants was the first fruit of his labours. It took the no.1 spot in *The Herald's* Children's Bestsellers chart during 2006, with *Lee Goes For Gold* no.4 at the same time. Keith never looked back. Out came *Lee's Holiday Showdown* followed by *Lee on the Dark Side of the Moon.* However, you can read the Lee novels in any order you like.

As well as writing, Keith now visits over 100 schools, libraries and book festivals each year and is renowned for his hilarious and energetic events. If you would like to invite Keith to visit your school, email him at:

keith@keithcharters.co.uk

This book is for:

Carrie & Rory

Moon facts

- The Moon is not as big as Earth, but it's still quite big.
- The Moon is a long way from Earth.
- The Moon is roundish.
- The Moon is not made of cheese (as many people think), it's actually made of solidified yoghurt.
- The Moon isn't attached to the Earth by elastic.
- No-one lives on the Moon, which is why the shops aren't very good.
- There aren't any trees on the Moon because someone chopped them all down.
- The Moon is in the sky. It's also in space.
- Moon aliens are terrible at juggling because they have 15 legs but no arms.
- There are the same number of sheep and cows as humans on the Moon.
- The best place to see the Moon is ... on the Moon.
- Mars aliens make confectionary, which they send to Earth for us to eat. Moon aliens don't.
- There is no Man In The Moon. It's a woman.
- The dark side of the Moon is ... darker than the light side.

There, you're an astronomer!

Chapter One

Wooooooooo-hooooooooooo!

Does it mean you're excited or nervous if your stomach feels like a washing machine on maximum spin speed?

That's what Lee wanted to know as he heard the Launch Director announce, *'Thirty seconds to lift-off.'*

It was easy for the Launch Director to be calm: he was sitting safely in front of some screens at a desk in the Firing Room; whereas Lee was strapped in alongside Captain Slogg and Sports Bob, his fellow astronauts. It was in their safe – and very large – hands that Lee's safety would rest during their attempt to reach the Moon.

'Twenty seconds ...'

Lee tried to think of all the things he'd been taught during his week's training. There had been so much to learn ... and so much to forget immediately afterwards.

'Ten seconds. Main engines ignited ...'

His mouth was dry. He hoped that his underwear would still be in ...

'Five, four, three, two, one ...'

Lee *felt* the roar as much as he heard it. The power was sudden and amazing and right underneath him, as if the world's most powerful Jacuzzi had been installed in his pants. Every part of him shook. He squeezed his eyelids shut to make sure his eyeballs wouldn't fall out. He didn't fancy having to feel about for them in the corner of the spacecraft.

Lee had been in the simulator and so expected lift-off to be like the moment a roller coaster reaches the highest point of the track and starts to dive, accelerating at breakneck speed. And it was a *bit* like that ... except with a huge bomb underneath. A bomb filled with thousands of litres of fuel that could explode at any moment if the technicians hadn't set up everything exactly as they should.

'We have lift-off ...'

For several moments Lee wanted to feel something solid, to be reassured that there was still a rocket around him. What if this was all part of a massive explosion that was sending him thousands of metres into the air only to plummet back to Earth a few seconds later?

Lee tried to turn his head to look at his fellow astronauts. Only he couldn't. Well, you try turning your head next time you're accelerating from standstill to

17,000 miles per hour in just eight minutes.

Seventeen THOUSAND miles per hour. Wow! Not only was he going to be the first kid in space, he was about to travel faster than anyone else his age had ever gone.

What worried Lee was the jolting and juddering. He imagined this was how it felt if you were caught in a strong earthquake. Captain Slogg had warned him to expect it, but he had not told him just *how* uncomfortable it would be. Every bone in his body felt like it was separating from its neighbour. He expected his head to roll off his shoulders any second.

Captain Slogg's calm voice filled his ears. 'You okay back there? Enjoying the ride?'

'Eh, yeah.' Lee could hear the breathlessness of his own voice. 'It's ... amazing!'

'Sure is.'

And it *was* amazing now that everything was okay - now that the launch had gone according to plan and there were no bits of him heading off in different directions to explore the outer reaches of the galaxy.

Lee grinned. He was officially THE FIRST KID IN SPACE. The first *ever*. No-one could take that honour away from him. He was chuffed to bits. There had been hundreds of photographers clamouring to take his picture before he set off. Thousands would want images of him when he returned. He would be famous around the world and ...

And what was *that?!*

The shaking had stopped.

Very suddenly.

Too suddenly for Lee's liking.

Had the engines conked out? Had someone forgotten to fill up at the pumps before they set off?

'Booster rockets separated,' Captain Slogg announced. 'We're on our way.'

Ah, of course. The solid rocket boosters had burned off all their fuel: despite the huge size of the boosters, it only took a couple of minutes to empty the thousands of gallons they contained.

Lee realised this meant they were already more than twenty-five miles above the ground, even though only two minutes had passed since lift-off. Twenty-five miles in two minutes! Plenty of his classmates back at school wished they could get to the front of the queue at lunchtime at that speed.

'Sit back and enjoy the ride,' Captain Slogg said. 'Next stop: the Moon. Would all passengers please have their tickets ready for inspection. Please note that only *return* tickets are valid on this flight.'

Chapter Two

'We're now officially in Earth orbit,' Sports Bob announced moments later.

'Already?' Lee was looking at the digital clock. They had taken off twelve minutes earlier.

'You bet. Now, one and half times around the Earth and we'll be on our way to the Moon. Plenty for us to do before then, but you enjoy the view.'

And what a view it was.

Lee blinked, then shook his head to wake himself. Orbiting Earth in a spacecraft ... being the first kid to go into space! What was he thinking of? It was clearly all a dream. His mind had wandered off while he was sitting at his school desk. It did that sometimes. Quite a lot actually. He was amazed that The Ogre hadn't shouted at him yet. Surely she'd noticed his daydreaming. She usually did.

Although for a dream it all seemed...rather real. The walls around him weren't covered in mathematical equations or diagrams showing the inner workings of the human body, but by switches and dials. And the pupils in the seats next

8

to him were much older than usual – adult age. One was fiddling with some controls. Lee couldn't recall there being any controls on his school desk. (He wished there were. It would certainly be handy to have a button that created a force field, or a lever that made teachers forget they'd set homework that needed handing in.)

It *felt* as if he was in space. It *looked* as if he was in space. Therefore ... he was in space. It was true. It wasn't a dream. He had to believe it now. He really was on a spacecraft heading to the Moon. It didn't seem possible and yet it was. He had won the right to be on this mission, just as the child who'd named the craft had won the right to have *Special Cosmological Research Astronaut Project* painted on its side in planet-sized letters, only there hadn't been enough room and they'd had to put the initials instead: *SCRAP*.

Won the right? Doesn't that suggest Lee entered a competition to become the first child on the Moon? Yes, well deduced. You'll make an excellent detective.

But Lee *win* something? How did *that* happen?

Eh ... luck. Pure, simple, can–you-believe-it luck. The competition had been on the back of a cereal packet and there'd been a mix up. The address to post the entries to had been printed as 666 Somethingorother Road instead of 999. But Lee had been looking at the address upside down. The result was that he was the only entrant. The same thing had happened with the naming of the ship. Well, almost the same. A massive two people had entered that. (And as the other entrant wanted it named 'My Dolly's Lovely Rocket' Lee was unbelievably glad that the judges had opted for SCRAP. Or, as Slogg and Sports Bob had nicknamed it, The Tin Can.

Anyway, that's all just a long way of saying that Lee was the luckiest person on the planet. Except that he wasn't on the planet anymore, he was orbiting it. But at least now you understand why.

Captain Slogg turned in his seat until he was facing Lee. He was wearing his serious face.

The captain was tall, with hair so short and blond he could easily have passed for a bald man. A few freckles clustered around his nose, and his eyes were as dark as black holes, though luckily much safer. Lee found it hard not to stare to see if there was anything in them.

It seemed that Slogg was the fittest man on the planet. Running, swimming, cycling, pole vaulting, egg and spoon racing ... you name it, Captain Slogg did it. He had run marathons, competed in triathlons and swum the Pacific with one hand. Or was it the English Channel single-handed? Lee couldn't quite remember.

However it was not because of his fitness that Slogg had been chosen to lead their mission, it was because of his experience. He had been into space twice before, once to the International Space Station and once 'flying around looking at probes' as he had described it to Lee. In fact, Slogg had gone space walking to fix a satellite that was in danger of crashing to Earth.

(Not that any of the above explains why he had his serious face on. But this next bit might.)

'Now Lee, I trust you've been paying close attention to everything you've been told during your training.' Lee nodded. 'Because it's lonely in space and we'll all be relying on each other. That means *we*'ll be relying on you just as much as *you*'ll be relying on us. I can't stress enough how important it is that you listen carefully.'

Lee nodded again. He would try his best to listen, though listening had never made it into his *Top 10 Things I'm Good At.*

Slogg continued. 'The worst thing would be to have someone aboard who doesn't listen properly. That would be awful. Can you imagine that? They could put everyone's life in terrible danger.'

Lee could listen more effectively, but he is a talented, intelligent boy who should go far. That was what it had said on Lee's best ever school report. (You should have read what the others said.)

And, in a way, how right that teacher had been, because Lee would soon be going *very* far - further than any other kid in the entire history of the human race. Not unless some had been whisked away in UFOs, but Lee thought that was unlikely.

'Aw,' Lee said to Captain Slogg.

'And danger up here is serious danger.'

'Right.'

'But I don't want to go on about how dangerous it might be. I'll scare you.'

The captain laughed. Lee didn't.

Two and a half hours later, and after Sports Bob and Captain Slogg had talked to Mission Control about a whole load of stuff Lee didn't understand, Sports Bob told Lee to hold on tight again – they were about to head for the Moon.

'The third stage engine will blast us out of Earth orbit and we'll be on our way again,' he said. 'Then, in about half an hour, we'll do some spinning around.'

'"Spinning around?"' Lee didn't like the sound of that. Lee thought that sort of thing was fine at a theme park, not tens of thousands of miles above the planet. 'Is that as in *spinning around out of control, oh man we're all going to die?*'

'No no no. Well I sure hope not! It's nothing to worry about. We need to separate our command module from the third stage, spin around so we can dock with the lunar module, discard the stage three engine, then we'll be off to lunar orbit.'

'Eh ... right,' Lee said. 'Maybe you could ... just tell me when it's all done?'

'It's all done,' Sports Bob said. 'Just over two days now and we'll be there. Next stop, lunar orbit. Now, who's got the cards?'

Chapter
Three

Now all they needed to do was keep on heading for the big rock floating in space. Meanwhile they could chill out a little and have some fun.

After a while Lee's nervousness subsided and his mind turned to other, equally pressing matters. Matters that were pressing more on his bladder than on his mind.

'Where's the toilet?' he asked. It had suddenly occurred to him that he hadn't been shown one during his training.

Captain Slogg glanced at Sports Bob before responding to Lee.

'Ah. The toilet, 'Sports Bob said. 'Well that will be a ... new and, ehm ... *interesting* experience for you.'

'Why? Is it really hi-tech?'

'Eh, no, I wouldn't say that, exactly. Did no-one show you how it works?'

'No.'

'Ah,' Captain Slogg said. 'Well that was a rather unfortunate oversight.' He rose from his seat and floated over to Lee. 'Come on, I'll show you, then you can give it a go.'

'Right,' Lee said, although he was thinking, *It's only a*

toilet. I know how toilets work!

Together Lee and the captain pushed themselves off the walls and made their way to the end of the capsule. Captain Slogg reached out for a handle and opened what Lee had assumed was a cupboard. It wasn't, probably because it was so small that nothing could be stored in it, but some bright spark had decided that it could still be used as a toilet.

'Now, Lee. This will be a bit tricky ...'

'I know, I will hardly be able to move in here, and I'm half the size of you.'

'What I mean is we're still in a zero gravity situation.'

'Aw.'

'So the procedures here are somewhat different to those back on Earth.'

'Yeah, you have to squeeze into a space built for a rake.'

'I mean in other ways.'

Captain Slogg described to Lee what those procedures were. 'The thing to remember about doing the toilet in space,' he said, 'is this: if *you* can float ...'

'If I can float ... what?'

Captain Slogg grinned. 'Try it and see.' And with that he closed the door.

Lee was left staring at what Captain Slogg had said he

would need to use: a plastic bag. A special plastic bag (according to the captain), but a plastic bag nonetheless.

Lee wished he had taken his mum's advice and not left it until the last minute; then he could have spent more time trying to figure out what he needed to do. As it was, he had waited longer than he ought and needed to move fast to avoid an embarrassing accident.

Quite why he needed to use a bag rather than a normal toilet Lee wasn't sure. He was convinced Captain Slogg was messing with him. Sports Bob and the captain would laugh their heads off if he peed into the bag instead of the toilet. Of course they would.

So Lee pushed his feet into the straps on the floor and started to pee into the toilet normally ...

... and immediately realised why Captain Slogg had told him not to.

Lee's pee didn't splash into the toilet. Instead, it floated. It became a rope of pee, hovering above the toilet in globules. A rope you would not want to climb.

Lee panicked, but once he had started to pee it was impossible to stop. Peeing is like that.

And so the rope of globules grew longer, stretching out in front of him, reaching for the wall like one of Spiderman's webs.

What was he going to do? He couldn't leave the toilet like this, it would be so embarrassing when either Sports Bob or Captain Slogg needed to go, which eventually they would. And what if he couldn't get rid of it and had to open the door? Would it float through the capsule for the whole world to see on TV?

So Lee decided he had to do something. And the something he decided to do was to chase his pee around and try to catch it in the plastic bag.

It wasn't as easy as he'd imagined. He couldn't move quickly in the weightlessness and the pee didn't stay still when he swung his bag to catch it. After a couple of attempts he tried another tactic, creeping up on the pee like a lion on its prey until the bag was right over it. Only then did he close the ends of the bag over it.

His new method was much more effective and it wasn't long before he had scooped up half a bagful. He was relieved, not because he stood a chance of setting the world scooping-up-pee-in-a-spacecraft record but because he could now leave the toilet.

He spotted a globule that had escaped. It passed centimetres from his nose, causing him to lean back to avoid it. He fell against the door, which was half open, and waited to crash to the floor, but it didn't happen. Instead, he somersaulted in the air, righted himself and swam back to the others. Weightlessness had its advantages as well as its disadvantages.

In the laboratory part of the capsule Captain Slogg was conducting an important scientific experiment. It involved precise measurement and would be of great interest to humankind. Yes, he was calculating how far through the craft he could reach with only one push against the back of his seat and without touching the sides. The answer was: quite far. And once he was moving he was unable to stop himself.

'Woah!' Lee cried as the captain bashed into him, bouncing him back into the toilet door he had exited seconds earlier. And 'Ow!' the captain cried as he caught the back of his head on a handle in the roof. He rubbed his scalp while screwing his face up like a bulldog's. 'That was sore.'

'You okay?' Sports Bob called back.

'Alive, thanks,' the captain called back. 'More importantly, I set a new record!'

'How did you get on in there, Lee?' Sports Bob called over his shoulder. He was concentrating on fiddling with knobs that did something Lee knew nothing about.

'Eh ...'

'Tricky, isn't it. But don't worry, you'll soon get the hang of it.'

Adrenaline kept Lee going for several hours. He watched what his fellow astronauts were doing, trying to learn as much as he could.

Lee worried about what Captain Slogg and Sports Bob thought of him. Years of training, perfecting all the tasks that need to be carried out on such a trip ... that's what *they* had gone through. By contrast, Lee had only been on a one week crash course (not that they were *intending* to crash, of course) and was worried that he would be a distraction – an annoying kid who kept getting in the way. It seemed to Lee that some adults thought most young people were annoying and got in the way. Those people had forgotten they had been young themselves once. Lee's teacher, The Ogre, was a good example, although it was at least two or three centuries since she had been young, so perhaps it was understandable that she had forgotten. She seemed to think Lee was annoying and in the way any time he was in her classroom.

Not that Lee wasted a lot of time thinking about all this. Time was precious. Why waste it thinking?

If it was easy to understand why Captain Slogg *was* in

charge, it was just as easy to understand why Lieutenant 'Sports Bob' Sleigh was not. Because Sports Bob was slightly mad.

Lee had met him on his first day of training. He was cheerful, with curly hair that grew outwards rather than downwards and a moustache that covered half his face. It was if he had stuck an otter across his top lip. He also had puffy cheeks and huge feet that made him waddle like a penguin.

When they had first met and shaken hands Sports Bob had told Lee, 'Lieu-tenant does not mean I live in a toilet.'

Bob was bonkers in general, but in particular he was bonkers about sports. He loved every sport ever invented, from football to cheese rolling and basketball to welly boot throwing, and knew all the rules as well as the latest results. He would surely have become a sports reporter had he not become a top astronaut.

You would imagine from his obsession with sport that Sports Bob would be just as fit as Captain Slogg. And you would be ... wrong. One look at Sports Bob left little doubt that he was an armchair sports addict.

As well as being a walking encyclopaedia of sport, Sports Bob was, according to Captain Slogg, a genius with the lunar module's knobs, buttons and dials. This was good news given that he would be flying them to the Moon.

Lee liked Sports Bob. He was able to see the inner Bob – the man hidden underneath the slightly odd outer Bob. Yes he was mad, but he was good mad, not bad mad like Hitler and others who give mad a bad name.

Sports Bob was also the trip's chief scientist, in charge of the many experiments loaded aboard. Lee didn't fully understand what the experiments were all about, but he knew some involved collecting samples from the lunar surface. Space geologists thought there might be water on the Moon, albeit underneath the surface, and the experiments Sports Bob would be in charge of would help scientists work out if this was true.

After a while Lee grew tired, there was no getting away from it. Though he only needed to remind himself that he was headed for the Moon and he would stop yawning and start feeling excited all over again. However, he knew (even without his mum having to tell him) that if he stayed up too long he would be exhausted come the morning ... or whatever time it was. It was hard to tell.

'I'd better go to bed,' he told Captain Slogg. 'While no-one else is trying to. It's not as if there's lots of room.'

'Okay. Well just remember that we're still in zero gravity. You can sleep any way around.'

Slogg led the way back into the sleeping area, with Lee following.

'*Any* way?' Lee checked.

'Any way at all. There's no such thing as a right way round now we're weightless.'

'Cool!'

'You okay to sort yourself out if I go back and join Bob?' Slogg asked. 'There's still plenty to do.'

Lee said he was and Slogg swam away, using one of the handles to give himself an initial push-off.

With Slogg gone, Lee had to make one of the stranger decisions of his life: to sleep standing up or standing on his head? He chose standing up – it seemed a little less weird.

So Lee climbed into his sleeping bag and leaned back against the bed. And Slogg was right, he lost any sense of which way was up and which was down when he closed his eyes.

He didn't expect to fall asleep quickly, but he did. And what a good sleep it was. He hadn't slept well during the nights before they blasted off, he was too excited. But now … ah, that was great, drifting off … drifting …

'Lee? You're drifting.'

I know, he thought. *It's great. The best sleep I've had in ages. Just drifting ...*

'Lee.'

Sshh. I'm sleeping.

And in that sleep it was as if he was being pulled silently through deep, soft snow by a team of reindeer. Or was he floating along a corridor? Floating and then ... bouncing off a wall ... and then off another wall? What a bizarre dream.

'Lee!'

And now the walls were talking and ... Ouch! What was that? The walls were attacking him now! It hurt in the dream.

And now he was turning around. Turning upside down and heading back down the corridor.

'I'll need to strap him in,' someone said. 'Did no-one tell him about that? We can't have him floating around the craft like this. He'll hurt himself, or bash into the controls.'

Finally Lee opened one eye slightly. And there was the back of Captain Slogg's almost bald head. Why was *he* there? And then something was being placed gently across his legs and arms ...

But none of it was worth waking up for.

When Lee did finally waken he found he had been tied to a wall.

This was a surprise.

Not a good surprise.

The craft had clearly been taken over by aliens who had tied him to the wall so they could torture him. There was no other explanation.

Lee wriggled and found that the aliens had done a hopeless job of tying him down. Maybe they didn't know how to tie knots where they came from. Whatever, he was able to slide his entire sleeping bag out from under the ties. He was free! Now to get off the craft.

Eh, no.

When he thought about it for a nanosecond he realised that getting off wasn't such a good idea. Not midway between Earth and the Moon.

If he couldn't leave The Tin Can his only other option was to overpower the aliens. Maybe that wouldn't be too hard. If they weren't good at tying knots maybe they wouldn't be much good at fighting either. Lee certainly hoped not, especially as all he had to fight them with were his bare hands.

Lee swam to the door and prised it open ever so slightly. He waited for someone or something to lash out at it. When that didn't happen he opened it a fraction more.

When he plucked up enough courage to peer through the gap he saw ... nothing unusual. Captain Slogg and Sports Bob were sitting in their seats, talking quietly. Or at least the backs of their heads *looked* like those of Slogg and Sports Bob. There was no way of telling if it was really them. The aliens might have taken over their bodies.

There was only one way to find out.

Lee opened the door enough to squeeze through and, as quietly as he possibly could, swam up to Slogg and Bob. All was going well until a sneeze ripped through Lee without warning. He had no chance to stifle or swallow it. A great big snottery mess flew out of him and floated towards his waiting hand. Nice!

The fright the sneeze gave Lee was nothing compared to the shock it gave Captain Slogg and Sports Bob.

'Woah!' Slogg cried, leaping from his seat. Or trying to. His lap belt held him down.

'What's with the creeping up on us like that, Lee?' Sports Bob wanted to know. 'And watch out with that snot, it's floating in my direction!'

Lee grabbed it from the air and wiped it on his trousers.

(Well, what else could he do?) 'Sssh!' he whispered. 'They'll hear you and know I'm free.'

Sports Bob and Captain Slogg both stared at him as if he had two heads, three arms and one hundred and four fingers, none of which was the case. 'Lee, what are you on about?' Sports Bob asked.

'Oh, and before I forget,' chipped in Captain Slogg, 'you need to strap yourself down when you go for a snooze. I found you floating around the craft in your sleeping bag earlier. I had to tow you back in to the sleeping quarters and fasten you to the wall. Didn't they tell you to do that in your training?'

'Eh ...'

'They really do need to revise their training manuals,' Sports Bob told Captain Slogg. 'They're supposed to cover all the basics, but they clearly don't.'

'So, nothing unusual happened while I was sleeping?' Lee checked.

'Nope. Apart from you floating around the place. That was a little odd.'

So, no aliens, no spacecraft being overrun. There was only one thing to be said, so Lee said it.

'Aw.'

Chapter
Six

❛ Hello Earthlings! Greetings from space. We are circling above your planet with our super-destroyer ray gun, ready to blast you into a million billion pieces. Our attack craft have your planet surrounded and are awaiting my command. Do as I say or we will take over your homes and schools.'

'What?' the children could be heard whispering to each other. But that only served to amuse the imperial intergalactic overlord, who continued to taunt them.

'If you do not complete your homework on time we will zap your planet with our mega ray and kill all who live on it.' He let out a sinister laugh, 'Ha, ha, ha, ha, haaaa ...'

'Lee ...' Captain Slogg started to say, but the overlord would not be thwarted. He was enjoying himself too much.

'We have enslaved the peoples of other planets, people who have disobeyed us. Do not make the same mistake, oh peoploids of Earth.'

There was a moment's hesitation before all of the gathered children smiled and called, *'Hello, Lee!'* waving as they did so. Even The Ogre waved, though she didn't smile in case her face cracked.

Lee was enjoying the eyes of the world being on him. It wasn't just his class watching, there were millions of others checking him out, waiting to hear what words of wisdom he would utter.

'I am not Lee. You think I am Lee, but actually I have taken over his body so that you will be less afraid.'

'Lee!'

Lee turned to Captain Slogg. 'What?'

'Maybe a bit less of the evil tyrant looking to take over Earth thing?' the captain whispered. 'The whole world is listening and watching.'

'Aw. Okay then.'

Lee faced the screen again. 'Earthlings, I was only kidding. Your planet is not in danger. Not unless anyone tries to beat my school hot dog eating record while I'm in space.'

'*So have you not really got a super-destroyer ray gun?*' asked Lee's classmate Ben.

'Eh, in a word ... no.'

'*Aw,*' most of Lee's class said at the same time, seemingly disappointed that Lee's body had not after all been cloned by an evil alien intent on enslaving the people of Earth or destroying their planet.

'*Does anybody want to ask Lee a question?*' The Ogre

encouraged the class. *'A sensible question, of course.'* She waited for a hand to be raised. None were. *'Doesn't anybody want to ask Lee a question?'* Still no hands. *'Any sort of question?'*

Asha's hand snaked up.

'Yes, Asha,' The Ogre said, relieved.

'Does pee really float in space?'

'Now, Asha, honestly ...' The Ogre reprimanded her.

But Lee thought it was a perfectly sensible question. 'Yes,' he told Asha, 'it does. At least for boys it does, but it might be different for girls. I don't know because I'm not a girl.'

'No,' the captain said. 'It would be the same. Gravity doesn't care if you're a girl or a boy, it's the same for everyone.'

'How do you know? Have you done experiments?'

'Well ...'

'Any other questions,' The Ogre encouraged, keen to change the subject.

'Have you landed on the Moon yet?' Lee was asked.

'No, not yet. We'll be doing that tomorrow morning.'

'Does Earth look small from where you are?'

'It does. It's hard to believe I live there, and that you're all down there. It's not like flying in an airplane. Well, I suppose it's a bit like that, only everything is much further away and way smaller.'

'Are we like ants?'

'You're not like anything because I can't see you. I mean, I can see you now, on the screen, but not out of the window.'

'Have you seen the aliens?' someone wanted to know.

'Aliens? What aliens?' Lee was momentarily spooked. 'On our spacecraft, you mean?'

'Anywhere. On your spacecraft, out in space ... wherever.'

'No. And I don't want to see any.'

'They might be friendly.'

'Or they might not.'

The questions were coming thick and fast now that someone had started the ball rolling.

'When are you coming back, Lee?'

'Not for ages. Not until ... Saturday.'

'That's not long.'

'We're just looking forward to having you back with us,' The Ogre said. *'We've been saving lots of homework for you. Maths, Spelling, Comprehension ...'* Her evil grin would have made any imperial overlord proud. And, come to think of it, she did look like an alien monster.

'Gee, thanks,' Lee told her. 'I can't wait.'

'Good.'

'Eh, I was joking.'

'Captain Slogg, how quickly can The Tin Can fly?'

And that was it, Lee's classmates all wanted to speak to the captain now. They could speak to Lee any time.

Chapter
Seven

Meanwhile back on Earth on the Breaking News show ...

'This breaking news has just come in ... Panic has set in across many countries following reports of aliens threatening to blast our planet with a super-destroyer ray gun. Reports say huge traffic jams are forming as terrified citizens try to flee to the country.

'The leaders of several cults have claimed that this is The End Of The World. However, this has been denied by the world's major governments. Over to our reporter, Ant Ena, outside the White House ....'

'Quick, we're off air now ... run for your lives!'

Before setting off, Lee had imagined he wouldn't be able to take his eyes off Earth for the entire journey. He would watch it become more and more distant until finally they orbited it. So he was surprised that after a while he grew used to seeing the blue, green and white planet behind them. Looking back at it was like watching a firework display: the first few blasts made you gasp, 'Wow!', but each one after that seemed a little less impressive.

It was partly that Earth seemed less real the further they flew from it. Now it merely looked as if a child had cut a picture from a book and stuck it on the black background of space.

The Moon had grown larger and larger as they had moved further from Earth. Lee stared out of the window but it was hard to judge the distance between the capsule and the barren, eerie landscape stretching out endlessly in front of him.

Although barren, the lunar landscape was not dull. A little voice in Lee's head kept reminding him that the surface they would soon land on was tens of thousands of miles from Earth. This was not like parking a car. A minor bump now would spell disaster, not a costly repair bill.

Eventually, after two days travelling through nothingness, it was time to leave the command module and enter the much smaller lunar module. It would take them down to the surface of the Moon, while the command module would continue to orbit on its own.

Captain Slogg had explained how technology had changed the way missions operated. 'The first time men landed on the Moon, one of the astronauts had to stay behind in the command module. He flew round in circles, while the other two got to walk on the surface.'

'No way! So he never got to walk on the Moon.'

'No. They called him the loneliest man in the universe. When he was behind the Moon there wasn't even any radio contact with Mission Control. He really was completely alone, two hundred and fifty thousand miles from Earth.'

Wow, all that distance from the Earth with no way of contacting anyone back home. Lee wondered how much it would cost to send The Ogre there.

'Our mission is different, though,' Slogg went on. 'We'll all be landing on the surface. This command module' – he pointed to what was around them – 'can be flown by remote control from the lunar module and from Earth.'

Which was impressive.

'We need to crawl to get into the lunar module,' Slogg said. 'You'll have no problem ... I'm not so sure about Bob. We may need to shove him from behind.'

Luckily Sports Bob did make it through the narrow gap that led to the lunar module, despite having to wear his space suit.

'It's the space food,' Bob said. 'It's not exactly appetizing. 'I've lost weight. Flying to the Moon is the best way of dieting I know. It's not as if I can nip to the shops for sweets.'

Soon they were in their positions and Sports Bob ran through a long equipment check, making absolutely certain that everything was working before they separated from the command module. Lee found this boring, but he didn't complain. He was as keen as the others not to find themselves drifting in space without any hope of rescue.

Excitement coursed through his entire body. This was the last stage of a long journey. Now all they had to do was land safely.

That thought was fresh in his mind when suddenly he heard a loud click. Lee leaned forward anxiously to ask Sports Bob what it was, only to find the pilot turning to face him. They bumped helmets.

'We have separation,' Sports Bob announced, recovering from the bash. 'A few hours and we'll be there.'

Lee assumed they would be heading straight for the Moon's surface. He was wrong. They needed to orbit the Moon first. Not once, but five times. Something to do with experiments, mapping and more equipment testing.

At last Captain Slogg spoke to Mission Control and they were cleared to descend. Gradually they flew towards their designated landing spot.

'Now remember, it may be a bit bumpy when we land,' Slogg told Lee. 'The runways up here are in a terrible state.'

As they drew nearer, the Moon filled their vision. Soon it was no longer a big chalky white ball in the sky but a surface below them, with identifiable features. Lee had never been to the most remote part of Earth, but he imagined that it looked something like the Moon.

'Nearly there,' Captain Slogg informed Lee, who was both surprised and worried by how fast they were still travelling.

'Have we got good brakes?' he asked.

Sports Bob nodded as he concentrated on finding somewhere to land.

Down further, flying close to the tops of craters, Lee could soon make out individual boulders on the screen above the main instrument panel. Some of them were big, the sort of big you didn't want to crash into.

'There's more here than I thought,' Sports Bob mumbled. 'Didn't think it would be quite so rough.'

Mission Control came on. *'Need to get down soon. You have two minutes and ten seconds of fuel.'*

'Roger.'

'Are we going to run out of petrol?' Lee asked.

Captain Slogg showed Lee his crossed fingers. That wasn't reassuring.

Another minute passed. Lee watched every one of the sixty seconds count down on the digital clock. And then he watched twenty more evaporate before Sports Bob turned round briefly with his thumbs up. 'Got ourselves a landing site.'

A few moments later the craft tilted back and slowed until it was almost hovering.

'We're going in,' Sports Bob announced. 'Ten seconds to touchdown. Hold on.'

Lee's heartbeat trebled its rate and his hands began to sweat. He didn't remember much from his training but he did remember that landing and lift-off were the most dangerous parts of any flight.

Captain Slogg seemed to sense Lee's nervousness. Grinning, he said, 'Don't worry. It'll all be fine. And then you'll be the first child ever to land on the Moon.'

Lee managed to relax his face just enough to grin back, although he imagined it was one of his scarier grins. Being the first child on the Moon: that really was something to look forward to.

'Five seconds ...'

Would the world's media be splashing his name all over their TV shows and newspapers? Was he going to be famous?

And then there was a bit more of a bump than Lee had been expecting.

The capsule wobbled.

'We're tipping over!' Lee cried.

Sports Bob was as cool as a fridge. 'Okay, hold on, we've hit a small rock.'

Small rock? Then how come it was tipping the capsule further and further?

Captain Slogg leapt from his seat, throwing his harness aside.

'Lee! Quick, get up!'

'Why?' Lee said, doing as he was told nonetheless.

Captain Slogg threw himself towards the raised side of the capsule. Lee immediately understood and did the same. He was a lot lighter than the captain but realised that a single gram could be the difference between them toppling over or staying upright.

The capsule hung at its limits, as if it intended staying there forever. Then it lurched in the opposite direction, sending Lee and Captain Slogg crashing across the floor. It bounced up again on the other side, then rocked a few more times before finally settling.

'Well, I apologise for the bumpy landing,' Sports Bob said. 'Circumstances beyond my control. But that's us, we've touched down. Captain, Lee ... Welcome to the Moon.'

They had landed on the Moon!

Lee grinned from ear to ear. 'Yes!' he said to himself, fist clenched in front of him. 'Yes, yes, yes, yes, yes.'

Sports Bob was milking the moment.

'Please keep your seatbelts securely fastened until the pilot turns off the seat-belt signs... Oh, you've taken them off already. Never mind. Lieutenant Bob Sleigh and his crew would like to thank you for flying on this rocket and hope that you will choose to fly with us again soon.' He added, 'Not that you have any alternative if you want to return to Earth.'

Again the voice at Mission Control was calm. *'Congratulations everyone. And nice flying, Bob. Sounds like you had some hairy moments there.'*

Through the loudspeakers they could hear cheering.

Captain Slogg and Lee shook hands then both took great delight in reaching over and slapping Sports Bob's back. Hard. Harder than was strictly necessary.

'Ow!' Sports Bob said. 'What do you think this is? A boxing match?'

'I can't believe we're actually on the Moon,' Lee said.

'Why, where did you think we were going to land? Uranus?' Bob grinned.

'So let's get out and explore!' Lee enthused, heading for the door.

'Not so fast,' Slogg said, shaking his head. 'First we've got to do some more checks and set up the experiments.'

'Aw,' Lee said. '*More* checks and experiments?' He was itching to walk on the surface.

Lee could barely believe how many experiments they were going to be undertaking. There was enough kit onboard to set up a small factory.

Although he had no idea what any of it did, Lee loved some of the fancy equipment, especially the Cosmic Ray Detector. He was amazed to hear that such a thing actually existed and couldn't wait to tell his classmates he'd been using one. 'I thought they were made up - for comics and films,' he told Sports Bob.

'Nope, they're the real deal. They take one on nearly every mission.'

Some of the bits of kit had really weird and wonderful names. There was an S-Band Transponder, an X-ray Fluorescence Spectrometer, a Bistatic Radar and a Lunar

Portable Magnetometer. All were powered by the Radioisotope Thermal Generator ... whatever that was!

'It's the battery,' Captain Slogg told him.

'Aw.'

'We just call it the Radioisotope Thermal Generator because it sounds good.'

He was right, Lee decided. It did sound good. He would practise saying it for when he returned to Earth. He might even shorten it to RTG so that it would sound as if he used one all the time.

'And Lee, now that we're here, remember it's extremely important that you follow to the letter any instructions I give you. This isn't a trip to the shops. We're on the Moon.'

'Explains the lack of trolleys,' Lee mumbled.

'What's that?'

Lee hadn't meant to speak out loud.

'Eh, I said I should have brought a brolly.'

Lee helped Sports Bob and Captain Slogg carefully remove more equipment from the cupboards. At the same time he remembered that he was now officially The First Child On The Moon. Cool! He would soon be in history books and people around the globe would come to know *his* name just like they knew the names of Neil Legstrong and Buzz Lightweight. Eh, no, that wasn't what they were called, it was... Buzz Lightyear? Buzz Oldyear? Buzz Oldyin? Heck, what was his name again? It was something like that. But they wouldn't forget Lee's name like everyone had forgotten whatshisname's, the astronaut who had stayed in the command capsule when...Headstrong...no, Armstrong, that was it...when he and ...Aldrin, yes, that was him - had become the first two men to stroll on the Moon's surface.

Then, once all the equipment was ready, there was the business of making sure their space suits functioned properly.

Lee and Captain Slogg checked that they could hear each other on their radios. 'Hunky Dory,' the captain told Lee.

'Loud and clear,' Lee told Slogg.

They made their way to the door.

Lee suddenly felt nervous. What if he floated away? What if he got lost? What if his air supply ran out? What if he didn't think *what if* quite so much? Actually, that was probably best.

Sports Bob said. 'All checks complete. You're cleared to leave the capsule. Ding ding, round one.'

'Yeehah!' Lee yelled.

'Calm yourself,' Captain Slogg told him. 'I know it's

exciting, but we're here to do a job. We have to be professional. We've got the experiments to conduct. We need to take soil samples and measure the solar wind, the emission of certain gases and the scattering of radar waves. And that's just for starters.'

'Aw,' Lee said, not for the first time.

Slogg held up the box he was carrying.

'Gamma-ray Spectrometer,' he announced.

Lee nodded. 'I thought so. Which TV stations can you get on that?'

Slogg chuckled. 'None on this version. We could only afford the basic model.'

'When you're quite finished,' Sports Bob said, 'you're clear to descend to the lunar surface,' he told them.

Excitement returned and crowded out Lee's fear. This was it. His moment of glory, the highlight of his life so far.

'Keep close,' Captain Slogg told him.

'I will. I don't want to get lost in the crowds.'

'And be sensible. Remember, the world is watching.'

Cool, Lee thought. The whole world was watching him as he readied himself to step on the Moon. Amazingly cool. Freezer cool.

The door opened. Wow. The surface of the Moon had looked awesome from behind the capsule windows, but now it looked ... real. And all that lay between him and it were five small steps.

Captain Slogg went first. One foot, then another, taking his time, moving carefully, getting used to the space suit and the limited gravity.

Lee watched from the top of the steps as the captain neared the bottom.

'Captain!' he called.

'Eh, what?' Captain Slogg lost his footing on the last step and tumbled to the ground. 'Ouch!'

'Oh, sorry. I didn't mean to distract you ...'

'I was thinking up something to say, something everyone would remember!' the unhappy captain snarled.

Sports Bob came on over the radio. 'Well, Captain, I think everyone will remember "Ouch!"'

Slogg climbed to his feet and brushed himself down.

Meanwhile, Lee looked back at the capsule in the way that someone about to dive off a high board at a swimming pool might look back to make sure no-one is about to give them a push. He gave the capsule a good hard look, as if he might never see it again. Then he put one foot in front of the other – more carefully than Captain Slogg had – until he reached the bottom step.

But as he stretched a foot towards the ground he

hesitated, realising that this was a truly momentous moment and that momentous moments called for momentous words. He scrabbled about in the dark reaches of his brain to come up with something original.

'This is one small step for man ...' he told the world, knowing that this wasn't at all original but that people might be impressed that he was about to repeat the famous – indeed momentous - words of Neil Armstrong, first man on the Moon. Except that he couldn't remember the rest of it now. Nerves were getting the better of him ...'One small step for man ...,' he repeated. 'Eh, one giant step ... for people with small feet.'

'Sorry, Lee,' Sports Bob called to him. 'We had a problem with your radio there and lost what you said. Can you repeat it?'

Lee was relieved. That hadn't sounded good at all. So he took the opportunity to say a few different words. He felt the weight of history on his shoulders (or was it a dusting of dandruff?). Whichever, he decided this was a time for serious words.

'Hello everyone, it's nice to be here on the Moon. We have a lot of hard work and important experiments to do using RTGs and cool Cosmic Ray Blasters ...'

And then over the radio Lee and everyone else listening

heard, 'Wheeeeeee ...' and when Lee turned he saw Captain Slogg springing across the Moon's surface. 'Boiiiiing ..... boiiiiiing .... boiiiiiing ....' he called with each new bound. 'Wow, this is brilliant, Lee!'

So much for being sensible, Lee thought. Unable to resist joining the fun for another second, he followed Captain Slogg, bouncing across the Moon's surface.

What an amazing feeling. Once he was off the ground it took him ages before he landed again. If only he could return to Earth able to jump in the same way. He would be school high jump, long jump and triple jump champion, easily.

A slightly crackly voice brought him back down to Earth. Or back to the Moon anyway.

'Lee, have you still got me in sight?'

'Sure have.' Lee turned around to see the captain, but turning wasn't so easy because the same atmosphere that allowed you to jump so high and so far also slowed you down when you tried to swivel your body.

'I bet you a shot at the capsule's controls I can jump further than you.' Captain Slogg challenged.

There was nothing Lee liked more than a challenge.

'Okay, you're on. Where will we make the starting point?'

Captain Slogg looked around and pointed. 'That big

round rock over there.'

'Alright, you go first.'

The captain took as good a run-up as was possible in a space suit when there isn't much gravity around, and launched himself.

It was a decent jump. But Lee had spotted something.

'That's not fair,' he complained to super-fit Slogg. 'You jumped from way after the spot we agreed. I get to add extra to my distance.'

'Okay, a little bit,' the captain conceded. 'Let's see how you get on.'

Lee backed up from the jumping line to give himself a bigger run up than the captain's, even though he wasn't really sure if it was worthwhile. Then he charged, working furiously to persuade his legs to move at anything like a run. It was almost impossible. He understood why the captain had been unable to stop himself jumping from beyond the line. He ended up doing the same.

Once airborne Lee tried to do what he'd seen Olympic long-jumpers do on television, throwing his legs out in front of his body ... until he realised his legs weren't satisfied with being in front of the rest of his body, they wanted to be above it. That left his body below his legs ... which meant he was upside down.

He was still that way around as he approached the ground. Lee braced himself for a painful fall, but he bounced as much as landed when he finally hit the surface.

In the helmet of his space suit Lee could hear Captain Slogg. 'That ... hahaha ... that was hahaha ... that was so hahaha ... That was the funniest thing I've seen in my entire life hahaha. Even funnier than the time I flicked the wrong switch when we were coming into land, hahaha.'

Lee was back on his feet in double quick time.

'You flicked the wrong switch when you were landing?' he gasped. 'What's funny about that?'

'Oh, it was just a little switch, it didn't cause any problems.'

'But it *could* have.'

'Only if it had been an important switch.'

'Was it *near* any important switches?'

'Lee, you've seen the flight deck. There are so many switches; it's not always easy to remember which one is which.'

'Eh...' But Lee was lost for words. What could he say to a spacecraft captain who had just admitted being unable to remember which switch was which on the flight deck ... the same spacecraft captain he was relying on to get him safely back to Earth!'

'Don't look so worried, Lee. We got here safely, didn't we?'

By now Lee had picked himself off the dusty surface for the second time in two minutes and was standing upright again. He suddenly remembered that people back on Earth would be listening.

'Hi everyone. It's so cool up here on the Moon. Hope you're enjoying the show. A special hello to any of my classmates who are listening. This is such a great mission to be on. I haven't had to do homework for two weeks!'

Lee laughed, thinking this was hilarious. He suspected his classmates would not be laughing quite so loudly.

They walked on towards a nearby ridge. Captain Slogg had decided to set up their experiments immediately below it.

'Do you think there is life on the Moon?' Lee asked.

It took the Captain a fraction longer than Lee would have liked before he replied. And even then it was with a, 'No. There probably isn't.'

'What do you mean, "*probably* isn't"? This is the Moon. I don't see any dodgy Moon aliens hanging around waiting to carry us off.'

'True. I can't see any either. And I think we'd have found out by now if there was life on the Moon. We've studied it enough. But who knows? Maybe we've missed the signs.'

'Look at this place though. What could live here?'

The Captain shrugged. 'Who would think anything could live in our deserts? Or around those boiling vents at the bottom of the seas? Yet animals and plants do. Life is amazing, Lee. I wouldn't be surprised if it existed on half the planets we've decided it can't possibly be on. It might not look like life as we know it, but I reckon it will be there, somewhere.'

The captain was staring out into the blackness of the universe, as if struck for the first time by the size of it. Lee stared as well. Not that there was much to stare at, but he stared anyway.

'So you do believe in aliens,' Lee said.

'Not exactly ...'

'You said there's life on other planets, but not as we know it. So you mean aliens.'

'Alien life forms is more how I'd put it.'

'So ... aliens then.'

'Whatever, Lee. Come on, let's head back.'

Their conversation was cut short by Bob, who had unexpected news.

'Hate to interrupt the party,' he said, 'but we've got company.'

'Argh! Aliens!' Lee cried. 'You were right, Captain!'

Meanwhile back on Earth on the Breaking News show ...

'More breaking news .... Fresh panic has hit the world, just as citizens thought their fears of an alien invasion were unfounded. Once again people are heading for the hills.

'It seems that the source of the panic has again been Lee Waters, The First Child In Space. It seems he was heard shouting that the SCRAP capsule was being attacked by aliens.

'Over to our reporter in Moscow, Mike Rophone ....'

'Yes, once again many cults have said this is a sure sign that the end of the world is nigh and that they didn't get it wrong last time it was simply a false alarm. Meanwhile governments around the world have denied that an alien invasion is imminent ...'

Chapter
Ten

Captain Slogg and Lee hurried back to the capsule. Well, as much as reduced gravity and a space suit allow anyone to hurry.

'No, not aliens,' Sports Bob told Lee as he and the captain entered the lunar capsule again. The lieutenant rolled his eyes as if they were a couple of marbles in his head. 'An unidentified rocket is heading this way.'

'Seriously?' Captain Slogg asked.

'Mission Control thought it was a satellite being launched when they first saw it. Turns out it's more than that. It's Erokea's first manned space mission. And they're really going for it. They're headed *here*.'

'Which country?' Lee asked.

'Erokea,' Sports Bob said. 'It's one of those breakaway countries. Always very keen to put itself on the map.'

'Why?' Lee asked.

'Because most maps don't show it.'

Captain Slogg scratched his head. 'But why here?'

'They could ask the same,' Lee pointed out. 'Why are *we* here?'

'Yes, but we're carrying out important experiments and

collecting samples and …'

'And because we can be,' Lee finished for him. 'We're showing off to the rest of the world.'

Sports Bob nodded. 'He's got a point there, Captain.'

'There's a lot more to it than that,' Captain Slogg argued. 'Some of the inventions required to carry out a mission like ours have major uses for people back on Earth, don't forget.'

'True,' Sports Bob said. 'But a bit of it is still scoring goals because we can. We've already won the game but we want to beat the record for the highest ever score.'

Captain Slogg reflected for a moment.

'Lee, the human race is always trying to move forward and discover new things. And I'm glad of that.'

Lee supposed he was too, otherwise he would not be on the Moon.

'When are they due to land?' Captain Slogg asked.

Sports Bob checked his watch. 'Mission Control estimates just another few minutes.'

'And would they prefer tea or coffee on arrival?'

Sports Bob smirked. 'I forgot to ask.'

'Does Mission Control know *where* they're going to land? Lee asked. 'Should we be putting on our hazard warning lights to make sure they don't crash into us?'

'The Erokeans haven't given us any co-ordinates. But they know we're already here because *our* landing was on TV.'

Captain Slogg shook his head. 'The Moon is turning into a car park. First us, then the Erokeans...'

Sports Bob had tuned out of their conversation and was listening intently to whatever was going on in his headphones.

'Captain!' he shouted, even though Lee and Captain Slogg were both next to him. They spun round. 'The Erokeans are in trouble. Listen.'

Sports Bob switched the radio transmission to the speakers so they could all hear Mission Control describe what they were witnessing back on Earth.

'They've got a problem with the thrust on one of their engines. The whole capsule has tilted to one side. They're ...' There was some frantic talking in the background before Mission Control continued. *'We believe they're going to crash land. They don't have full control of the craft.'*

'A *big* crash landing?' Captain Slogg asked.

'Could be.'

'Close to us?'

'No. They were always targeting somewhere on the other side of the Moon. Seems that's still the case. Hang on, their

mission control is through to us again.' After some babbling the voice returned. *'Well, well, well. They've asked if you guys can be on standby to assist if necessary. I didn't think those Erokeans would ever ask the outside world for help. That's a first.'*

'It makes no difference who they are,' Captain Slogg said in his best superhero voice. Maybe that's why he was super-fit; he was superhuman. 'If they're astronauts in difficulty we'll do our best to help them. They'd do the same for us, I'm sure.'

'Okay, they're on their final approach ... swinging around all over the place ... Woah, that doesn't look good. No no no. Oh, they've got it straight again .... Oh, no they haven't.'

Lee, Slogg and Sports Bob listened intently, experiencing every moment as if they were with the Erokeans on their spacecraft, which they were glad they were not. They knew what it felt like to be thrown around; their own landing had been less than smooth.

'They don't have control over where they're going to land. This is going to be one interesting touchdown.'

'How far from us do you estimate they're going to end up?' Captain Slogg asked.

There was a short delay before the mission controller replied. *'Could be ten ... even twenty kilometres.'*

Lee was watching Captain Slogg's face for any indication of how serious the situation might be. By the looks of it, it was grim.

'That's quite a distance,' the captain observed. A moment later he asked, 'How far will the moon buggy's battery take us?'

He was asking Sports Bob, but it was Mission Control who answered.

'It should get you there if it's fully charged.'

'And what about getting back?'

'You'd need to recharge the battery when you got there.'

'Have they got a recharger?'

'Don't know. We'll check for you once they've touched down. Assuming they'll tell us.'

Captain Slogg said to Sports Bob and Lee, 'There's not much point heading over there if we can't get back.'

Lee had other thoughts on his mind. 'What are we going to do once we get there?'

The captain shrugged. 'Whatever we can. It depends how it all works out for them. It could be okay. Then again ...'

Lee knew what the opposite of okay was.

The speaker crackled again as Mission Control came back online.

'Into final descent ... They're wobbling all over the place ... Last fifty metres now ... They're coming down faster than they should be, and still sideways ...'

Lee and Captain Slogg stood riveted to the radio transmission. This was not like a faulty plane landing at an airport. There were no fire engines on standby, waiting to assist the crew to safety and a nice cup of tea. Those astronauts were on their own, relying entirely on their skill and training to get them safely onto the Moon's surface.

'Thirty metres to go ... Woah, swinging around a bit wildly there ... Ah, nice correction, they're straight again ... Twenty metres ... Their TV pictures are giving us a view of where they're going to land now. I doubt that's where they intended. Oh-oh, they've got some big rocks under them. They're going to have to watch those landing feet.'

No-one spoke. They were all listening closely, no thoughts of rivalry with the other astronauts, only concerns for their safety.

'Five metres. Firing on the left for balance ... Or they were. Unbelievable. It looks like one of the other engines has gone too!'

Sports Bob was living every second of the Erokeans' plight. 'Just one booster working. Man, this is going to be seriously ropey. They must be all over the place. It's like trying to win a game when half your team have been sent off.'

'It's like trying to balance a pyramid on one corner,' Captain Slogg told Lee. 'It won't do what they want for more than a few seconds.'

'Come on!' Lee shouted at the speaker, wishing it made a difference but knowing it didn't.

'They've swung left … They've swung right …'

'Sounds like they're doing the Hokey Cokey,' Sports Bob mumbled.

'They're coming down on their side as far as we can tell.'

'Keep her straight,' Sports Bob called. He was swinging his hands from one side to the other as if fighting the controls of the Erokean spacecraft.

Captain Slogg shook his head. 'They're going to roll when they hit the surface,' he predicted.

'Ah now, what's going on … We've lost communication with them … No pictures, no sound … We're trying to get it back.'

Neither of the men said anything. And for once in his life Lee kept quiet too.

Mission Control was sombre.

'Still nothing. By our reckoning they must be on the surface by now.'

Lee could not hold back any longer. 'Have they crashed?'

'More than likely,' Captain Slogg told him. 'And from the height they were at ...'

'You mean they're all dead?' Lee interrupted, shocked. 'Dead on the Moon?'

Mission Control came back through. *'We've just had word from the Erokeans. They can't raise them. They've lost all contact, audio and visual. All they've got is a locator.'*

'But that is still working?'

'Yes.'

'Well, that's something. It means their capsule wasn't *totally* destroyed by the impact.'

'Where has it landed?' Captain Slogg asked Mission Control.

'We'll try to get you the details.'

After a couple of minutes Mission Control replied with what to Lee was a jumble of numbers. To his fellow crew members they were precise co-ordinates.

Captain Slogg and Sports Bob checked a map.

Slogg sucked air in through his teeth for several seconds once they had identified the spot. 'That's a long way off course. A long long way. They were supposed to land ... well, not exactly on top of us, but not too far from here.'

Bob raised his eyebrows. 'Good thing we didn't bump

into them.'

Captain Slogg grimaced. 'And what's worse is that they've landed on the other side – on the dark side.'

'The dark side?' Lee repeated. 'Like in Star Wars?'

'No, Lee. The Dark Side of the Moon.'

Chapter
Eleven

'So it's dark where they are now,' Lee checked, 'but it'll get light again and warm up for them?'

'It will, but not for a good few hours. It's just turned dark where they've landed because they went so far off course.'

'So how are we going to help them?'

'That's a very good question. The Erokeans will want to do this themselves if it's at all possible,' Captain Slogg declared.

'What?' Lee asked. 'Why won't they ask for help to save a crew stuck up here?'

Sports Bob answered him. 'Because that's what the Erokeans are like.'

'I don't understand,' Lee said. 'They're like ... what?'

'Lee, what do you know about Erokea?' Captain Slogg asked.

'Eh ... not a lot.'

'It's a very secretive country. It's run by a dictator who lives in luxury while half his country starves. He thinks that buying weapons to threaten his neighbours is more important than feeding his people. Anyway, the point is that he tries to avoid foreigners whenever he can.'

'Lee was appalled. 'But what about the astronauts? He can't leave them here to die! *We* can't leave them here to die.'

'We won't, Lee. Not if there is any way we can avoid it.' Captain Slogg was thinking positively now. 'There's a chance they've made it down in one piece, in which case every minute could make a difference. So we need to get to them as soon as possible.'

Sports Bob was more cautious. 'I agree we should investigate if we can, but we shouldn't hold out too much hope. They were swinging about all over the place. I wouldn't fancy trying to land this craft without two of the three main thrusters, I'll tell you that without a half-time team talk.'

'Bob, Lee, there must be a way of rescuing them. We've just got to work out what the way is. So let's get our thinking caps on.'

So, while Mission Control made their own calculations, Captain Slogg, Sports Bob and Lee tried on a variety of vividly coloured caps in an attempt to come up with some bright ideas of their own.

Thirty minutes passed. Lee could have sworn those minutes lasted longer than usual, as if the Moon's lesser gravity was slowing time the same way it slowed footsteps.

Seconds seemed to hang in the air, unable to march with their usual regularity.

Finally, Mission Control came on the line once again.

Captain Slogg held up his hand for silence in the capsule.

'Okay everyone, here's the story. Good news and bad.'

'Let's start with the bad,' Slogg said.

'Okay. The bad news is that the Erokeans don't have any sort of back-up craft they can send to rescue their guys. That much we had already guessed. And they still don't have audio or visual contact with their craft.'

'No surprises there,' Sports Bob said.

'The slightly better news is that their readings suggest the crew managed to get the craft onto the surface without destroying it completely.'

'So there's a possibility they've survived,' Captain Slogg said.

'A possibility. No more than that.'

'Then we must attempt to reach them.'

'That's going to be a problem, Captain.'

'Why?'

'They'll accept our help - frankly, they can't stop us. The problem is your moon buggy. That vehicle is intended for short journeys. Its batteries aren't designed for long distance rescue missions. And those guys are quite a way

65

from you. You would make it there, but you wouldn't make it all the way back. You'd end up stranded in the middle of nowhere.'

This was not what they wanted to hear.

'So what are you proposing instead?' Captain Slogg asked.

'Well,' the mission controller said, *'so far we haven't come up with an alternative.'*

Lee was shocked. 'You mean we're just going to let them run out of air or food or water?'

'Hopefully they may be able to repair whatever's broken. Then they might be able to attempt a lift-off.'

Sports Bob shook his head. 'That's going to be some task,' he said.

Captain Slogg scratched his considerable chin, Sports Bob rubbed his.

Lee left his chin alone and put his energy to more productive use. 'There might be a way,' he muttered.

Two expectant heads turned towards him, and those two heads suspected several more were leaning towards the speakers at Mission Control.

'We need to find a way of making the battery last longer,' Lee began. 'Well, the lighter we can make it the further it will be able to travel. And you're both quite heavy ...'

'I wouldn't say heavy …' Captain Slogg and Sports Bob said at the same time.

The captain was still looking at Lee, who wondered if he had some food on his chin or a stray bogey hanging from his nose. In fact it was neither, Lee discovered after checking, so he carried on.

'Mission Control's calculations are all based on the captain driving the buggy, yes?'

The two men nodded.

'Well, I'm the lightest one here. By quite a bit.'

The mission controller was shocked. *'Lee, are you seriously suggesting that you should drive the buggy? That you should go on a solo rescue mission? You haven't even passed your driving test!'*

'Only because I haven't sat it yet. I'll pass first time, no bother. You should see me on my bike. I can do wheelies and everything.'

'But there's no call for wheelies here, Lee,' Mission Control said. *'A solo mission is …'*

'… Is the only way of reaching those astronauts.' Lee was adamant .

Sports Bob let out a long, loud breath. 'No. No, we can't do that.'

Captain Slogg gave Lee the most intense stare he had

ever known. It was so strong that Lee felt it could have been used to make objects move across a room. 'Are you sure?' he finally asked him.

If on Earth someone had suggested he should go for a drive in the moon buggy Lee would have jumped at the chance. Riding around on one of those contraptions would be so much fun. However, he only had to look at the faces of Captain Slogg and Sports Bob to know how extremely dangerous a mission to a far off part of the Moon could be.

Lee tried to put himself in the position of the Erokeans. Assuming their ship had survived the impact, they were probably contemplating a long, slow, airless death a quarter of a million miles from home. And that wasn't good.

Lee took the deepest breath he had ever taken. Deeper than those needed to swim a length of his local swimming pool. Then he let that breath out, which took quite a few seconds.

'It needs to be done,' he stated simply. 'So I'll do it.'

Chapter Twelve

The buggy was stored in four sections. Lee helped Captain Slogg carry them down the steps and they laid them out on the Moon's surface.

Lee stood back and looked at them. One section had a name down its side. 'The Bugster,' Lee read. 'Cool.'

Captain Slogg managed a smile, his first since they'd heard about the Erokeans.

'Moon buggies are a lot smaller and lighter than they used to be. Technology has moved on. And it's precisely because they are so light that the weight of the driver makes all the difference to how far they can travel before the battery needs recharging. Anyway, wait until you see it built. I think you'll find it's not as bad as you're expecting.'

Lee and Captain Slogg assembled The Bugster. It was easy; a few turns of the spanner and it was done. And it was a lot better than Lee imagined. It had the look of an old racing car.

Captain Slogg proceeded to give Lee the fastest driving lesson in history.

'Press that for go, that for stop and turn the wheel to change direction.'

'Right ...' Lee waited for the rest of the instructions but they didn't come.

'That's it,' Slogg said. 'Lesson over. But you'd better practice before you head off. We'll recharge the battery to full immediately before you go.'

'Okay, so ... press this for go ...' The buggy shot forward, taking Captain Slogg with it because he was still holding on to the steering wheel. 'Woah ...!' he cried.

'Oops.' Lee hurriedly corrected his mistake. 'This to stop ...' Lee discovered the brakes were very powerful as the buggy came to an abrupt halt. However, Captain Slogg slid along the lunar surface for several more metres before ending up in a heap.

'And ... turn this to change direction ...' Lee checked. He didn't *mean* to press the accelerator again, his foot had a mind of its own. Before he knew it The Bugster was speeding towards the captain. He only just managed to apply the brakes in time, pulling up centimetres short of the captain who was yelling 'Lee!!!' into both of their helmets.

Lee apologised as Slogg climbed back to his feet. 'Sorry, it's the first time I've ever driven.'

'Who could have guessed?' the captain muttered. 'Well, you're going to have to learn quickly. *Very* quickly. You might as well try again. Get used to the steering, that's the most difficult part. I'll stand well back this time.'

So Lee did try again, taking the buggy further … and away from Slogg. And after five minutes he felt he was starting to get the hang of it.

'You're doing okay,' Sports Bob encouraged him, looking out from the capsule. 'You'll make it into Formula 1 yet.'

It wasn't a lot of practise but it would have to be enough. Captain Slogg topped up the charge on The Bugster and then he was ready to go.

'Remember,' Slogg reminded him, 'only brake if you really need to. It uses up energy to get going again and you need to save as much as possible for the journey back. Don't go racing off either. Take it steady.'

Lee tried to make himself comfortable in the buggy's seat, ready for the long journey.

'And don't forget,' the captain went on, 'we'll be in touch with you over the radio. Avoid large rocks and don't turn too sharply in case you roll.'

It was like Lee's mum speaking to him as he set off to stay at his Uncle Raymond's farm. The only thing Slogg had not reminded him to do was wash his neck regularly, brush his teeth at least twice a day and say please and thank you.

Lee looked out at the rugged Moon landscape. His feelings about it had changed. It had seemed so beautiful when they had first landed; now he thought of it as dangerous, a slumbering monster.

And it was with that thought, and a 'good luck' from the captain, that Lee trundled The Bugster slowly down the far side of a ridge and out of sight.

Chapter Thirteen

Everyone had been so focused on organising the rescue mission that Lee hadn't had time to feel nervous. Which was probably a good thing. No time to think meant no time for second thoughts.

Now, concentrating on driving had the advantage of taking Lee's mind off what he was going to do when he reached the Erokean craft. Indeed, off what way it might be sitting: upside down, right way round, sideways ... and that was *if* it was still in one piece. Lee realised he might arrive to find a scene of destruction, whatever the telemetry indicated.

Captain Slogg had warned him of this. 'Lee, you might arrive to find a scene of destruction,' he had said, 'whatever the telemetry might indicate.'

A riot of thoughts competed for attention at the forefront of Lee's mind - a crowded place at the best of times.

Lee had assumed the Moon would all look the same, but as he steered his way through gullies and around boulders he realised the landscape varied enormously, just as Earth's did. Some areas were flat and empty, others were hilly and rock strewn.

The biggest difference was the lack of green. Lee had never before missed a colour as much as he did now. He wondered if explorers attempting to reach the North or South Poles of Earth felt the same. Did they long to see a few blades of green?

It was difficult to know what sort of progress he was making; there were no signposts on the Moon. So Lee had to rely on Sports Bob, who let him know his distance from the co-ordinates he was heading for.

The further he travelled the darker it became. Holes tried to swallow him and rocks seemed to appear out of nowhere. He could not afford to take his eyes off the ground ahead, and after a full hour he found his eyes starting to close themselves. Twice he had to swerve hard to avoid an obstacle that earlier he would have seen before reaching it. Worried that he might have an accident, and that he could hardly pull up at an emergency telephone and call a tow truck if he did have one, he radioed in that he was going to take a short rest.

Lee stopped on top of a ridge. On Earth it would have been a path along the side of a river. On the Moon there were no rivers, just craters of emptiness.

The Bugster switched itself off when not moving, so Lee

did not have to worry about wasting energy while stretching his legs. A few leaps would soon get his circulation going again and stop his bum going numb.

Boing ... boing ... boing ...

Lee still got a huge thrill out of bouncing across the surface of the Moon because it was something he would never be able to do on Earth.

Boing ... boing ... boing ...

Oh yes, it was great fun.

Boing ... boing ... boing ... woah .....!

In his enthusiasm for boinging Lee had boinged one boing too far. Over the ridge he went. Luckily it wasn't far to the riverbed that wasn't a riverbed, and fortunately he landed softly because of the lack of gravity, otherwise he might have done himself a serious injury. He rolled to soften his landing, then stood and dusted himself down.

A voice filled his ears. '*Are you okay, Lee? Did you hit something?'*

'Eh, just taking a close look at the soil,' Lee said. 'Thought I ought to while I've got the chance. It's not every day that ...'

Lee stopped speaking.

Lee stopped doing anything other than breathing. He needed all his concentration to allow his brain to process what his eyes thought they had seen.

There had been a movement on the top of the ridge. Hadn't there? He was sure there had. Only ... how could there have been? What could have moved? There was nothing on the Moon except his fellow astronauts and the Erokeans, and they might not even be alive.

Unless it *was* them! Could they have crawled out of their craft after it crashed? Could they be trying to make their way towards Lee's craft, realising it was their only hope?

Maybe. However, if it was them, wouldn't they show themselves? Surely they would be desperate to contact the only other living beings on the Moon.

Lee kept his eyes peeled. (It made a change from the potatoes his mum sometimes got him to do.) He focused on the top of the ridges where he had, he was convinced, seen the movement.

Only when he failed to spot anything there did he scan down the slopes.

Still nothing.

Lee instinctively raised his hand to rub his tired eyes. Of course he ended up rubbing his helmet because it was in the way. The helmet also meant he was unable to scratch the annoying itch just below his left ear.

Again he scanned the ridges and slopes. Was he

imagining things, was that it? Were his nerves getting the better of him? Was he going doolally?

Lee wanted to say something to Captain Slogg and Sports Bob, but what would they think? That he was scared? That he was starting to see things that didn't exist? That he really was going bonkers?

'Don't be silly,' he whispered to himself.

'What's that, Lee?' Sports Bob called into Lee's helmet.

'Oh, eh ... Just talking to myself.'

'You want to watch out for that, Lee. First sign of madness, so they say.'

He was not going mad. And he was not going to go mad. He couldn't. The lives of three Erokean astronauts depended on him.

Lee took one more good look at the landscape around him, but there was still nothing unusual to be seen, just a dark horizon of rocks and moondust. He shivered as he realised if anyone - or anything- was watching he was hard to miss in his white space suit and fishbowl helmet.

However, before Lee returned to The Bugster he gathered together a small mound of rocks to mark the spot where he had - he was still certain - seen something move. He bounded back (in a more restrained way, having learned his lesson) and climbed aboard, but before he had travelled more than five metres, he was momentarily blinded by a flash of light.

It lasted only a fraction of a second and then was gone, but it was enough to set Lee's nerves jangling again. Had it been the dimming sun reflecting off a boulder? Had it been the buggy's lights doing the same? Or had it been something else altogether?

He reversed, travelling back the five metres he had come, following the same tracks. Nothing shone in his eyes. And when he drove forward again the light was still absent. But something wasn't right, and although Lee drove on, he looked over his shoulder at least once each minute.

Chapter
Fourteen

An hour later he rounded a huge boulder at the exit of a gorge and The Bugster's dim lights reflected off a metallic surface.

It was the Erokean spacecraft.

Or what was left of it.

Bits of metal once attached to the craft were scattered either side of a clear line. Lee assumed it had hit the ground and rolled, which must have been a terrifying experience for those inside.

Along its flank was some writing Lee didn't understand. Not only were the words different but they were written in letters Lee hadn't seen before. It had to be the spacecraft's name, but since he couldn't make it out Lee decided to call it The Dictator Ship.

He reported back to Sports Bob and Captain Slogg, describing the sight before him.

'That doesn't sound good, Lee. If they've rolled, the crew could be very seriously injured. I hate to say it, but they could even be dead.'

As Lee drew closer the scars on the spacecraft's body became increasingly apparent. It had taken some serious punishment and he was careful to avoid the debris strewn around the crash site. He could not afford a puncture.

When he reached the craft he stopped The Bugster and moonwalked around the capsule. The door was on the opposite side.

'Hello? Hello? Is anybody in there?' he called.

'Don't think they'll hear you with your helmet on,' Sports Bob told him. *'Likewise you won't be able to hear anyone calling back.'*

The solution was simple: take off his helmet.

And die within seconds.

So not the best of ideas.

Lee could see the door handle. He tried a couple of boings, but couldn't reach it. So he picked up a rock and held it in one gloved hand. He placed his other hand on the Erokean capsule, then banged the rock against it. He could feel the vibrations travelling through the metal body and into his hands. He tapped three times, then waited, hands still resting against the hull. It felt silly to be knocking on The Dictator Ship's door. It was like chapping on a friend's door to ask if they wanted to come out to play. But what else could he do?

Maybe they're trying to find something to bang back with, he convinced himself. Or maybe they were scared senseless that some*thing*, rather than some*one*, was trying to get into their capsule. A Moon alien, perhaps, intent on turning them into astronaut stew.

However, Lee was patient. Again he placed his hands on the craft and banged with the rock, then waited. Seconds ticked by and he decided that he was right - that it was not working. He let out a long sigh that caused his visor to cloud up.

Lee turned to The Bugster for inspiration. Was there anything on it he could use to force open the capsule? Anything long enough to enable him to reach the catch? Could he remove part of it? And if he did, would he be able to fix that part back into its rightful place afterwards?

He pondered this while leaning over The Bugster. Which was when something grabbed his shoulder. Something strong. Something fearless.

Lee screamed.

Chapter
Fifteen

Every nerve in his body exploded with fear. He leapt. His heart leapt. His brain leapt and hit off the top of his skull.

Woah! Aliens! He *knew* he'd seen movement back at that riverbank-without-a-river. Now he would pay the ultimate price for not having checked it out properly.

During those fractions of a second his life flashed by him. It didn't take long because he was still young, but what a lot he'd packed into those few years: being born (although he couldn't remember that), learning to walk (okay, he couldn't remember that either), learning to talk, going to school for the first time, eating his first hotdog for lunch, and his second, and his third ... setting the school hot dog eating record, going to the hospital to meet his sister Rebecca for the first time after she was born, returning to hospital when his appendix exploded, attempting to set up his business empire, being flooded out of the tent on holiday and blasting off from Earth. All of it in just a fraction of a second. It's amazing how so many memories can be crammed into so little time. But when your life is in mortal danger you have to think fast.

Lee thought very fast. Faster than he'd ever thought in his whole, short existence.

He turned as he landed from his leap, ready to defend himself. Whatever life-form was attacking him he would fight back. He wouldn't go down without a fight. He hadn't trained in Tae Kwon Do for no reason.

He spun round. It was a slow spin in his space suit, more a graceless twirl than the surprise attack of a martial arts warrior, but it meant he was now facing the beast that was trying to overpower him.

It was smaller than him and covered in silvery white armour. A bulbous helmet protected its head as it grasped at him. Inside that helmet was a wild, grinning face, eyes bulging.

'Man alive!' Lee cried into his helmet.

It mouthed something in response, but Lee couldn't hear it, nor could he lip-read .... Hang on, it had lips ... and a nose ...!

'Lee! Lee!' It was Sports Bob. *'What is it? Are you okay?'*

'There's something here, it's got hold of me, it's ... aaarrrggghhh ... it's a ...'

'What Lee? What?'

'It's a ... GIRL!'

'Lee, calm down now. You're seeing things, it's been too

much for you, you're exhausted. Now, look again and tell me what you see.'

Lee took a further look to be absolutely certain his eyes weren't deceiving him.

'Definitely a girl. She must be about the same age as me. What's SHE doing on the Moon? *I* was supposed to be first.'

'*A* woman *you mean.*'

Lee took a further look to be certain. 'No, it's definitely a girl. Roughly my age, I'd say. And ... she's got what looks like a small flag on her suit.' Lee described it.

'Ah, yes, that's the Erokean flag. You've found them. Well done. So, how is she?'

'She seems well enough. She must be to have crept up on me like that. She scared the life out of me.'

It took some waving of arms and raising of thumbs, but Lee managed to work out that the girl astronaut had plenty of bruises, but nothing broken as far as she could tell. However, the capsule's pilot had suffered at least one broken rib. Or that's what Lee *thought* he was being told.

The girl waved for him to climb in to the capsule. She climbed in ahead and stretched out a hand to help him. He could manage fine by himself but decided it would be churlish not to take it. She was only being helpful.

Inside, Lee was greeted by the other two Erokeans. They were ecstatic that he had arrived. 'Thank you, thank you,' they said as Lee removed his helmet. The second Erokean slapped Lee's back, but the third could not stand up and winced with each breath as he spoke. 'Thank you, thank you,' he said too, followed by what Lee presumed were words of welcome and relief, only they were in Erokean so he could not understand them.

Lee could see the surprise on their faces that he, a boy, was the one who had been sent, so he did his best to explain about the weight in The Bugster.

The Dictator Ship capsule was similar to the one Lee had landed in: lots of buttons and switches but not much space. It was not, Lee considered, a place *he* would like to spend his last days and he had no doubt the Erokeans felt the same. Their faces said more than words ever could. Even their delight at his arrival had not ironed out the worry on their foreheads.

Lee pointed to his chest and said, 'Me, Lee. Who you?'

'Ah, Me Lee Who You,' repeated the girl he had met outside, as if it was his name.

'Me Lee Who You,' the other two repeated too.

Lee realised he was confusing them and shook his head.

'No no,' he explained. 'Me, Lee.'

'Ah,' all three Erokeans said together. 'Me Lee.'

'No, no. *Me,* Lee.' He jabbed his finger at his chest some more.

'*Me* Lee,' the Erokeans stressed, still not getting it.

Lee sighed. This was going to be tough. He decided not to argue the point any further and instead tried to find out the Erokeans' names. He pointed at the girl who had given him such a fright outside.

'Sun Hee Wan,' she said, prodding her own chest.

'Ho Chin,' the less injured man told him.

'Po Kwan,' the pilot groaned up at him in two short breaths.

Working out what was wrong with The Dictator Ship was difficult, but after many hand signals Lee eventually reported back that he thought they were telling him that its thrusters had malfunctioned at the critical moment, just as Mission Control had suggested. It had left the pilot unable to steer properly. He had landed the craft as well as he could, but it had rolled two or three times.

Captain Slogg was impressed that they had managed to land it at all. *'The other two crew members owe their lives to that pilot,'* he told Lee.

There was no way of fixing The Dictator Ship. It was a wreck, even worse than the old annexe at Lee's school, which was saying something. And even if it could have been fixed it was almost upside down. Plus, the pilot was the one most seriously injured.

All of which meant that Lee would have to take them back with him.

'I feared as much,' Captain Slogg replied when Lee told him. *'Our craft is designed to carry three people, not six. It's going to be a tight squeeze. And it's not only the space that's a problem. It's the weight. It's like The Bugster: we can only carry so much given our fuel load.'*

'But we can't leave them here ...' Lee started to tell the captain, before remembering that although he had his earpiece in he had his helmet off and the Erokeans could hear what he was saying, even if they might not be able to understand it fully. So he smiled, hoping it would convince them that everything was okay.

'Lee, I'm not saying that we should leave them. We have to bring them back. Can you manage to bring the injured man back first?'

'I'll find a way. I'm sure the others will help.'

'We'll decide what to do after that. Oh, and bring some food back if you can. We don't want to starve. And make sure you haven't used up too much power getting there. At least if you make it back this time we'll know you can

make it there and back again.'

Lee wished he could see Captain Slogg smile as he said this. If he could he might not have felt quite so nervous about the *'if'* in 'if you make it back'.

Lee set about trying to explain to the Erokeans what it was Captain Slogg was proposing. They nodded their understanding then talked amongst themselves. The injured pilot shook his head and pointed to each of the others in turn. Lee realised they were arguing over who should go first and that it could go on for a while. So he waved his hands to stop them and pointed decisively at the pilot.

'Po Kwan,' he said. 'You're going first.'

Sun Hee Wan and Ho Chin nodded their agreement. The pilot would go first, whether he liked it or not.

'Thank you, Me Lee,' Po Kwan said.

Manoeuvring the injured Po Kwan onto The Bugster was difficult. All movement was painful for him. Even breathing was uncomfortable.

Sun Hee Wan, as the most able-bodied, tried her best to minimise the discomfort by insisting on slow, gradual movements as they lowered her injured colleague to the surface. They rested for a moment to give Po Kwan a chance to recover before they started on the next stage. If this was what he was like trying to get onto The Bugster, what was he going to be like on the journey back? Lee couldn't afford to travel too slowly - that would use up more battery than travelling at a steady speed.

Lee felt responsibility weighing heavily on his young shoulders. Only a couple of weeks ago he was an ordinary school pupil. Now he was about to become an ambulance driver on the Moon. It was not the sort of job careers advisers tended to suggest, but how quickly life can change.

Eventually, and with only one more serious 'oof', they lifted Po Kwan onto the buggy. Lee was relieved. Po Kwan mouthed something through his visor. Lee realised it was,

'Thank you, Me Lee,' again.

Lee took it easy to begin with. He wanted to make sure Po Kwan was able to keep himself in position on the passenger seat. The soft suspension of the buggy certainly helped. It ironed out most of the minor bumps but there were a couple that caused The Bugster to jolt and Po Kwan tightened his grip on the side of his seat.

'Sorry,' Lee mumbled, but the only people who could hear him were Captain Slogg and Sports Bob.

'Everything okay there?' Sports Bob asked.

'As okay as I can make it,' Lee replied.

And that was the best he could do.

'You're approaching half time,' Sports Bob told him.

Lee checked his moon watch. Sports Bob was right. And if he was approaching halfway he must also be approaching the place where he was so sure he had seen movement and where he had left the pile of stones.

He again tried to convince himself that he couldn't possibly have seen anything, but he failed miserably and scanned the horizon intently ... just in case.

Which was when he saw it. Again.

Chapter Seventeen

Dust rose from the surface like a miniature smoke signal, it seemed to be coming from just over a small ridge.

Freaky. And scary. Lee's back was suddenly very damp with nervous sweat. He glanced over at Po Kwan, but the injured astronaut was lost in his own painful world, unaware of anything going on around him.

Surely all he was seeing was the lunar wind blowing up some dust. Wasn't it? But it didn't make sense that such a wind would only affect one spot. Why wasn't the wind blowing dust around everywhere?

Lee slowed The Bugster and steered it towards the dust cloud. He was being drawn towards it like iron filings to a magnet.

Then, as quickly as it had appeared, the dust settled again and he had nothing to aim for. If he had been on his own he might have investigated further, but he had a badly injured passenger to consider. Po Kwan's wellbeing had to come before satisfying his own curiosity.

As he was turning the wheel, setting the buggy back on course towards the capsule, out of the corner of his visor he spotted a burrow.

Well, that's what it looked like. If he had been back on Earth it would have been easy to explain: rabbits. But he wasn't aware of rabbits being able to build and launch spacecraft, or of them having the space suits and helmets required to survive on the Moon.

So if it wasn't rabbits, what *had* caused this burrow?

Back on Earth there were hot springs, some of which shot water high into the air, turning it to steam. Could this be a Moon version of one of those? Did the Moon have a boiling molten core that bubbled to the surface now and again through cracks in the outer shell? Lee had no idea but made a mental note to check with Captain Slogg and Sports Bob when he made it back to the capsule.

Off he set again, bouncing along even though he tried his best to drive smoothly. After a further hour the capsule came into view.

Captain Slogg met Lee a short distance from the steps. He touched gloved hands with Po Kwan, avoiding shaking so he would not hurt him unnecessarily. Then together Lee and the Captain manoeuvred Po Kwan to the steps.

'Well done,' the captain told Lee. 'You deserve a medal.'

Lee agreed and wondered what it would look like. Maybe he could design his own - the Lee Medal for Exceptional Bravery on the Moon. He fancied one of those. He could take it to school to show his classmates. They weren't impressed by much, but surely they would be impressed by *that.*

Captain Slogg discussed with Lee how they would attempt to lift Po Kwan into their capsule.

'Can't Bob help?' Lee asked.

'No, he's not allowed to leave the capsule. Imagine if he locked the door and forgot to bring the keys out. We'd be stranded.'

The captain had a point.

It was even more of a struggle lifting Po Kwan into the capsule than it had been easing him out of the battered Dictator Ship to The Bugster. It would have been harder still had it not been for the reduced gravity.

Despite their best efforts they caused Po Kwan yet more pain. By the time they eased him inside he was paler than the first snow.

Despite this, Po Kwan still found the energy to mouth, 'Thank you, Me Lee.'

'I'm worried about him,' Lee confided in Captain Slogg once they were at the other side of the capsule.

'Why?' asked Captain Slogg. 'Because he can't say your name properly?'

'No, no. Because he looks terrible. He's ... he's not going to die, is he?'

'The journey has knocked the stuffing out of him, but we didn't have any choice. And at least now he can speak with the medical people. They'll soon work out what's wrong with him.' Captain Slogg pointed to the sleeping area. 'Bob and I will take care of him. You grab some sleep. You must be exhausted after all that driving.'

Throughout the journey back, and while lifting Po Kwan into The Tin Can, Lee had not allowed himself to think about being tired. However, now that he *was* thinking about it he discovered he was wrecked. 'Yeah. I can hardly keep my eyes open.'

'It's all that staring straight ahead. Strains the eyes. Go and lie down. You'll feel a lot better for it.'

So Lee did, although he had to sleep in one of the fixed chairs because the one and only reclining chair had been given over to Po Kwan.

Not that this prevented Lee from sleeping. Far from it. Within five minutes he was out for the count.

It seemed like a very short count, because five minutes after that he was being shaken awake again.

'Wh ... what? What is it?' he asked.

'Sorry to butt into your dreams, Lee, but it's time to get going again,' Sports Bob told him. 'Ding ding, round two.'

'Already? How many minutes have I been asleep?'

'Eight hours worth of minutes. Exactly four hundred and eighty of them.'

'Eight ... What?'

'And your snoring was terrible,' Sports Bob added.

Lee sat up. At home, back on planet Earth, he was not the greatest at rising in the mornings. Rebecca was a lot better than he was. She bounded out of bed, instantly full of energy and wanting Lee to play with her, even when it was only six o'clock. The sooner that girl learned to tell the time properly the better.

This morning was different though. He had something important to get up for. He had two more lives to save.

Sports Bob had rustled up some breakfast. Or, to be more accurate, he had added water to some flavoured powder.

'Yum,' Lee said, looking at it with no enthusiasm whatsoever.

'Tastes better than it looks,' Sports Bob told him. 'I promise.'

'That wouldn't be difficult,' Lee retorted. 'It couldn't taste any *worse* than it looks. Not without being poisonous. But I'll give it a go. I'm starving. I could eat a horse.'

'Ah, that's lucky, because it's powdered horse that I've made, especially for you. It's a space flight delicacy.'

What worried Lee was that there was no way of telling if Sports Bob was kidding or not, at least not by looking at the so-called food.

Lee tasted it gingerly (even though there was no ginger in it).

'It's a bit like ...' He recognised the flavour but was struggling to put a name to it. 'Like ...'

'Horse? Because you tend to find that powdered horse does taste like horse.'

'No, no. It's like ...' And then Lee's brain worked it out. 'Strawberries. And brown sauce. And beans. Yes, strawberries, brown sauce and baked beans. And ... chocolate?'

Lee shook his head but continued eating. Actually, it was not too bad, despite the unusual mix of flavours. How could some powder and water taste that good?

He scoffed the whole lot, despite his misgivings. He would need all the energy he could muster for what lay ahead.

In fact he found out after breakfast that the plan was for him to make both of the remaining trips in a single day.

'It may mean we can head back a day earlier. And frankly, Po Kwan could do with that,' Captain Slogg said quietly. 'He's not in a good way. He needs to be in a hospital where he can receive some proper medical attention, not stuck in a cramped spacecraft with a bunch of amateur first aiders like us.'

Lee glanced at the injured pilot lying back in a seat, eyes closed. Slogg was right, he didn't look good.

'Feel up to that?' Captain Slogg checked. 'It's going to be a long day for you. But at least once this one's over we'll all be in the same place.'

This hit home to Lee the urgency of the situation. Without any further delay he jumped into the familiar seat of The Bugster and set off.

Chapter
Eighteen

Lee's second journey to The Dictator Ship was easier than his first, but no less tiring. He knew what to expect and the miles passed without incident.

Sun Hee Wan insisted on playing Rock, Paper, Scissors with Ho Chin to decide who would go next. At first he refused, insisting that now Po Kwan had been dealt with it was women and children next ... or at least girls. But Sun Hee Wan was having none of it. She refused to budge until he played. Eventually he gave in ... and then lost. And so it was that Ho Chin joined him for the return trip, unhappy about leaving Sun Hee Wan behind. But she just smiled no matter what Ho Chin said. Lee had noticed that smiling was something she did a lot. It was as if it didn't matter to her that she was stuck on the Moon with a wrecked spacecraft and injured pilot.

Eventually, after repeatedly asking what Lee thought must be Erokean for, 'Are you sure you'll be okay?' Ho Chin climbed out of The Dictator Ship and sat huffily in The Bugster. He was definitely still not happy about going next.

Lee climbed in to the driver's seat and gave a questioning thumbs up. He received a half-hearted gesture back, but it was enough.

They set off. Ho Chin was, understandably, better company than the badly hurt Po Kwan. Although Lee was still unable to hear anything his passenger was saying, the Erokean was at least able to nudge Lee's arm occasionally and point out interesting parts of the landscape. Having Ho Chin beside him was like having a tourist guide as a passenger.

Lee was determined to turn around and go straight back to The Dictator Ship after transferring Ho Chin safely, but Sports Bob insisted he rested his eyes for at least twenty minutes. He insisted to the point of placing a towel over Lee's eyes to stop him concentrating on what was going on around him.

'No team stays out on the pitch at half time. They go to the dressing room for a pep talk and to recharge their batteries.'

So, a little over twenty minutes later Lee was back on the road. Or back on what he supposed was now the nearest thing to a road on the Moon.

Lee had confidence in The Bugster by now. He had used less of the battery on the second trip because he had been able to maintain a steadier speed. He had not had to slow to avoid the sorts of bumps that would have caused Po Kwan intense pain.

There was no reason why this last journey should not be similar.

Or no reason that Lee knew of.

And so, as he drove, he repeated to himself: *Two down, one to go. Two down, one to go.* It kept him focused.

Since Sun Hee Wan was last off and considerably smaller and lighter than the previous passengers, she indicated that she would like to bring a few extra items - personal knickknacks she and her fellow astronauts had brought with them to remind themselves of their families back home. There was nothing heavy, so Lee decided there was no harm in it. There had been plenty of battery power left after the second journey. He nodded his approval.

'Thank you, Me Lee,' she said.

Lee just smiled. He liked Sun Hee Wan. She had a bright face that radiated sunshine like the ... eh, Sun. Lee thought it was a pity she didn't live closer so they could be good friends.

Of course you needed to be alive to be friends. So Lee

suggested they set off for The Tin Can without waiting any longer.

Sun Hee Wan seemed emotional when the time came to leave the capsule once and for all. She patted its dented side one last time, as if saying goodbye to a pet dog. Even although it had been a bumpy landing to say the least, it had brought her to the Moon. Now it would remain as a monument to a failed mission.

Observing her sorrow, Lee tried to cheer up Sun Hee Wan by bounding over to The Bugster and attempting to do the splits in mid leap.

Doing the splits on the Moon was impressive. But it was also dangerous, because at mid stretch Lee let out a ripper. It wasn't deliberate, it just happened. There was nothing he could do about it.

And it was loud. So loud that he felt sure most of the universe had heard it. And quite a bit of it had – as we'll discover shortly. Lee was certainly sure that Sun Hee Wan must have heard it. That was embarrassing in front of a girl he was trying to impress.

What? Hang on. No no no no. He wasn't trying to *impress* her, just ... cheer her up ... honestly.

Anyway, if she had heard it she was too polite to say and climbed in to The Bugster alongside Lee. She was clearly brave as well as polite.

The problem with farting in a space suit is that once you've done it there is no escaping it. Which is bad news if it's a stinker, as Lee's was. It can't leave your space suit. If it could, that would mean there were holes in your suit, in which case you'd soon be a goner. And you can't leave your space suit until you get back to the capsule ... at which point you pollute the capsule.

So Lee was stuck with it. He'd have to drive the whole way back with the air he was breathing smelling of ... Let's just say it wouldn't be refreshing.

Meanwhile back on Earth on the Breaking News show...

'Breaking news just in ... Millions of people who were returning home after the false alarm regarding an imminent alien invasion are turning round once again. Space watchers say a massive explosion has been detected in the area of the Moon, close to where the Erokean spacecraft recently crash-landed. The cause is as yet unknown. Scientists say that such explosions are unheard of in that part of the Moon and that the explosion was so loud it blew their headphones off their ears. Over to Tokyo

where we join our reporter Mal Odorous ... Mal, this story is causing quite a stink.'

'Yes, cult leaders are now saying that this is without a doubt absolutely definitely undeniably categorically unquestionably and positively the end of the world this time. They say it's because people around the world have refused to believe them or give them lots of money.

'Meanwhile governments around the world are saying the cause is probably entirely natural ...'

Chapter Nineteen

Weariness had crept up on Lee on the way to pick up Sun Hee Wan. All that driving back and forth was exhausting. However, he felt revitalised now that he was on the last leg of his journey. *Nearly done,* he now repeated. *Nearly done.*

He was travelling faster now that he was more confident about his driving. And with the end in sight he was starting to enjoy himself again.

He was even starting to recognise places on his journey. One group of rocks looked like the ruins of a house. Another reminded Lee of those stone circles in which his Uncle Raymond said human sacrifices used to be made. ('Children who didn't tidy up their rooms properly or who didn't eat all their greens,' according to his uncle.) Either that or they were used for telling the time before watches were invented, though those stones would have been heavy to carry around on wrists.

There was even one rocky outcrop that was full of holes. Lee wondered if this was what people had seen from earth that had caused them to think the Moon was made of cheese .

It was shortly after Cheese Rock (as he now thought of it) that Lee and Sun Hee Wan passed his pile of rocks. Or rather what he had left as a pile of rocks. Because it wasn't a pile any more - the rocks were scattered.

Surely even one of those miniature dust storms he had heard about could not have blown them down. And Lee refused to believe that he had not built the pile well enough. He was a skilled and experienced pile-of-stones builder. He made or added to cairns every time he reached the summit of a mountain with his dad. What had gone wrong this time?

One hundred metres later he found out.

It was as they descended into a shallow crater that Sun Hee Wan suddenly grabbed Lee's arm.

He swerved, almost causing The Bugster to roll.

'Woah! What? What is it ...?'

She was pointing frantically. 'Over there, over there,' she seemed to be saying.

Lee strained his eyes, following Sun Hee Wan's finger. She was pointing towards ... nothing. Or nothing that Lee could see. He shrugged his shoulders to convey his confusion.

But that only made Sun Hee Wan even more insistent. She jabbed ahead of him, leaning so far forward she was close to falling from the buggy. But still Lee could not work out what he was supposed to be looking at.

Then it moved.

It very definitely, absolutely certainly, without a shadow of a doubt moved.

At first Lee blinked, thinking his imagination was playing tricks again. It was good at that. However, Sun Hee Wan was watching him. She was nodding, her eyes also questioning, saying, 'You've seen it too?'

Lee nodded back before rapidly turning his focus to where he had seen the movement. What had made it? What had glinted in the distance? Was it something in a rock, something like quartz back on Earth? But that would only explain the glinting. It didn't explain the movement they were both convinced they had seen.

And then it glinted again. And again. It kept on doing so, each reflection more intense than the last. Because it was drawing closer.

Now they could see an outline. And ... another to the left of the first.

Woah! Two of them. Whatever *they* were.

Two, and then three. And then four.

And then more.

'Captain!' Lee yelled into his helmet.

'You okay?' Sports Bob asked. *'The captain is ... otherwise engaged. He's ... inspecting the toilet facilities. That powdered food is creating havoc with his ...'*

Lee cut him off. 'Bob, there's life up here!'

'Good one, Lee.'

'Seriously, Bob. It's coming towards us! Right now!'

'What?'

'Five of them ... no, make that six.'

'Six what?' Sports Bob's tone had changed. No more joking. It was the first time Lee had experienced Serious Bob.

Lee gawped at the advancing outlines, trying to make them out. It was hard. The limited light was behind them, revealing only shapes, not faces or limbs.

'They're ... some sort of ... I don't know ... Moon Beasts ... like rats or something. I only know they're coming for us!'

'Rats? Beasts? Are you sure?'

'Absolutely sure.'

'And they're definitely not just being friendly? They might have a different way of showing it. They're aliens, remember.'

It wasn't something Lee needed reminding about.

'Exactly! And why would they be advancing on us if they're friendly? I'm certainly not waiting around to shake hands. Not that they've *got* any hands!'

More and more appeared, all of them heading towards The Bugster. They had it covered on three sides, leaving only one way out. Lee realised that if they did not make it through that single gap they would be surrounded, prisoners. That was, if Moon beasts even took prisoners …

Sun Hee Wan tugged Lee's arm again and pointed behind them as frantically as before. Yet more beasts were coming after them from that direction. And still more from the other side, moving and yet hardly seeming to touch the surface.

'There are dozens of them!' Lee called to Sports Bob. 'They're everywhere.'

'Be careful! Don't take any chances.'

Lee wasn't. He had never been more scared in his entire life. Maybe these creatures were delighted to see them and were rushing to say hello … or maybe they were in attack formation. That's what it looked like and Lee had no intention of hanging around to find out the hard way.

Neither had Sun Hee Wan. She was pointing from the Moon beasts to the accelerator, urging Lee on.

'We're getting out of here!' Lee yelled to Sports Bob.

'Go, Lee! Go!'

In his desperation to escape, Lee pressed the pedal so hard that the wheels spun on the loose surface, throwing up clouds of dust; they couldn't see a thing. Lee eased off the accelerator and they lurched forward slowly. The dust began to clear revealing a terrifying sight … the beasts had gained on them … two were within ten metres of The Bugster and he could see them much more clearly than he wanted to.

'They're Moon rats,' he yelled to Sports Bob. 'They're armoured, completely covered in metal. Like armadillos. And they've got vicious-looking teeth too.'

'Friendly or not?'

'Put it this way: I don't want to be kissed by one of them.'

Lee urged the buggy to greater speed, pressing his foot to the floor. 'Come on, come on!' he yelled at it.

Sun Hee Wan was holding on tight, but somehow managing at the same time to pull her legs and arms away from the sides in case a Moon rat fancied a quick bite to eat.

'This is amazing! You two are the first to see life anywhere other than Earth!'

A great honour, Lee was sure. But he would happily give it up to be safely out of reach.

'You haven't got too far to go. Keep your foot on that accelerator.'

'I am!' Lee hissed. 'I am! But it won't go any faster!'

Out of the corner of his visor he suddenly saw a single Moon rat coming at them from the flank. He calculated that it was going to plough into the side of The Bugster if he kept on at the same speed. It would be like a torpedo slamming into the side of a ship.

Sun Hee Wan had seen the torpedo rat too and was banging on Lee's arm. Lee nodded to let her know he was aware of the danger.

The rat was attacking from the left. Ahead, on the right, was a rocky outcrop. Lee kept on regardless of Sun Hee Wan banging his arm harder and harder. Then she covered her face, anticipating the impact. Lee still ignored her, keeping the accelerator pressed hard to the floor until the very last second. Only then did he slam on the brakes for the briefest of instants.

The torpedo Moon rat tried to slow itself but it was too late. It couldn't stop and instead slammed straight into the rocky outcrop.

Kaboom! The Moon rat exploded into a thousand Moon rat pieces.

'Argh! They're not rats, they're machines!' Lee yelled.

'We're being attacked by machines!'

This gave their attempt to escape a whole new dimension. And it was no use waiting for them to rust because they wouldn't: that needed air and moisture and the Moon had neither. No, they needed to get out of there faster than a barefooted man needs to get off boiling coals. Burningly fast.

They were in a crater and the only escape route was straight ahead. It wasn't especially steep, Lee had managed it before, but then he hadn't had a mechanised Moon rat attack to contend with. Lee had to slow the buggy as they climbed the slope. It was either that or risk flipping over. The Moon rats had no such problem; suddenly one drew level with the rear tyre on Sun Hee Wan's side and sank its razor-sharp metal teeth into it. Lee felt The Bugster judder.

Sun Hee Wan urged even greater speed, quite liking the idea of staying alive, but it was speed the buggy did not possess.

The Moon rat sensed victory. Still keeping up with them, it lunged again, and then once more, each time narrowly missing its target.

Just as it made another attempt, the buggy suddenly reached the top of the slope and regained full power.

Gradually Lee was able to increase the distance from the determined attackers.

Sun Hee Wan gave the international sign for 'phew', wiping a hand across her brow. Or at least across her helmet in the place her brow would have been if she had not been wearing her helmet.

'How far have we still got to go?' Lee checked with Sports Bob.

'Just over two miles.'

Lee swerved to miss a rock, sliding The Bugster round it like a rally driver.

'What *are* those things?' he asked Sports Bob. 'Have you any idea? Do Mission Control know?'

'Negative, Lee. No-one has a clue. There isn't supposed to be any form of life on the Moon. The folks back home are very excited about your discovery.'

Lee was sure they were. He could imagine the headlines:

THERE *IS* LIFE OUT THERE!

ASTRONAUTS DISCOVER ALIENS!

This was momentous. It was the sort of news that would cause people to remember exactly where they were when they first heard it. Eating their dinner. Eating someone else's dinner. Having their dinner eaten by their dog. Being confused and accidentally eating their dog instead of their dinner. Whatever, they would not forget it.

Lee shuddered as he imagined another headline ...

MOON RATS ATE OUR SON!

Meanwhile back on Earth on the Breaking News show ...

'More breaking news just in ... Lee Water's, the same kid who sparked off the fears of an alien invasion, has now said he's seen Moon rats, which are apparently chasing him towards the SCRAP capsule. What? Who writes this stuff? Can you believe this kid? This isn't breaking news it's ... something he's made up. Even the End of the World nuts haven't commented this time, so let's not bother going over to any of our reporters anywhere around the world.

'Instead, in celebrity news, one of the country's top authors, Keith Charters, appeared in court today charged with repeatedly including terrible jokes in his books. The judge let him off with a warning on this occasion, but said Charters should seek to make amends. In a statement to

*the media afterwards Charters said he would happily make
amends, although he wasn't sure what they looked like so
if someone could email him a diagram ...'*

It was becoming increasing difficult to steer The Bugster.
The tread on the tyres had been worn down in the
desperate bid to escape. Twice he nearly crashed into a
rock; he was forced to slow.

After yet another check over his shoulder to make sure
there were no Moon rats in sight, he tapped Sun Hee Wan's
shoulder and let the buggy roll to a halt. A second later he
was checking it for signs of damage and it did not take a
mechanical genius to determine the problem.

Sun Hee Wan shook her head dejectedly when she
realised the problem.

'Can you see us on your radar?' Lee asked his fellow
astronauts.

'Roger.' It was Captain Slogg this time. *'You're making
good progress. We'll soon be able to see you. You've only
another eight hundred metres to go.'*

'We *were* making good progress, Captain. Not any more.
We've got a puncture!'

' We need to walk,' Lee told Sun Hee Wan. Of course, the Erokean could not hear him. So Lee walked his gloved fingers in front of her.

Sun Hee Wan got the message and they set off, bounding across the moonscape as quickly as they were able, looking back over their shoulders every few boings. As they drew within two hundred metres of the capsule a Moon rat approached at speed. It was easily the largest they had seen, twice the size of the others and twice as scary.

Lee and Sun Hee Wan waved desperately at each other and tried to boing even more quickly across the lunar surface. They were eating up the remaining metres to the capsule, but so was the Moon rat. And now it was not alone.

'We're not going to make it!' Lee screamed to Sports Bob.

'Yes you are, Lee. Run!'

'I *am* running! I'm going as fast as I can in this stupid suit.'

Sun Hee Wan was slightly ahead of him. Lee was impressed at how quickly she was managing to boing with legs about the same length as his. Each boing took them three or four metres closer, but in the time they made those leaps the Moon rats covered eight or nine metres.

Another desperate look over his shoulder showed Lee just how close they were now. They stood no chance of making it in time. They were going to be caught. Lee remembered those metallic teeth. If they could rip open the tyre of a buggy, what would they be able to do to his flesh? Or to his space suit? If that ripped he would be a goner.

'Bo-oooob!' Lee yelled. He was panting. A few boings were one thing, but trying to bounce over such a distance, and at such speed, was exhausting.

Fifty metres to go.

The steps of the capsule were lowered.

Forty metres.

It was nearly upon them.

Thirty metres.

It was right on their heels.

Twenty metres.

It pulled up beside them.

Ten metres.

It overtook them.

Three metres.

The Moon rat stopped in their path, blocking their way.

It bared its shiny teeth.

Stand off. They were so close now and yet those stairs, a mere three metres ahead, seemed as far away as Earth.

Lee and Sun Hee Wan stared at the Moon rat. The Moon rat stared at Lee and Sun Hee Wan. Nobody – and nothing - moved.

Without warning, Sports Bob tumbled out of the capsule. Presumably his intention had been to climb down the stairs, but instead he fell forwards, arms outstretched to try to soften his landing ... and landed right on top of the rat. It was subjected to the full and considerable weight of his stomach.

Bob lay there for several seconds then carefully raised his stomach a few centimetres, then a few more. Actually, he had to raise it several more centimetres after that as well before the Moon rat was revealed beneath him.

Lee watched for any signs of life. Sports Bob was showing a few; the Moon rat wasn't. And that was the way Lee preferred it.

'Is it ... dead?' Lee asked.

Before Sports Bob could answer, Sun Hee Wan cautiously – and bravely - placed a hand over the Moon rat's back.

Nothing.

She extended her whole gloved hand over it and tightened her grip.

Still nothing.

Then she lifted it.

'It *is* dead,' Lee said.

Still holding the Moon rat as if it might explode at any moment, Sun Hee Wan turned it over.

'No wonder they can move so quickly,' Sports Bob observed. 'Look!'

It was only because he was staring at it that Lee believed what he was seeing. Caterpillar tracks. The sort tanks used.

However, there was no time to be curious. Less than a hundred metres away a horde of Moon rats was approaching.

'I can't fall on them *all*,' Sports Bob cried. *'Inside! Quickly!'*

Lee didn't need to be asked twice. He leapt onto the first step and bounded up the rest two at a time. Sun Hee Wan was close behind him, and Sports Bob dragged himself up at the rear.

It was only as Sports Bob made it into the capsule and slammed the door behind him that Lee realised two things. First, Sports Bob had made it onto the Moon's surface after all. Lee was delighted for him. And what better excuse for having gone against orders than that he needed to save Lee's life. Second, Sports Bob was carrying the Moon rat under his arm.

'Woah!' Lee cried. 'You can't bring that on board! What if it comes back to life?'

'Research,' Sports Bob told him. 'Important scientific research.'

'But it could be carrying a deadly virus.'

'Lee, it's not a living thing. It's no more likely to be carrying a virus than our space suits are. But we might put it in quarantine anyway, just to be on the safe side.' Sports Bob opened a cupboard, placed the rat inside, then locked it firmly.

Captain Slogg didn't even shake Sun Hee Wan's hand before commanding, 'Quick! Grab your seats. We're preparing for lift-off.'

'Already?' Lee said. 'I thought ...'

'We're under attack.'

'Attack?'

Sports Bob's jaw dropped. Lee caught it and handed it back.

Sun Hee Wan greeted Ho Chin and checked on Po Kwan, who was already strapped into a chair. There was some urgent conversation then everyone jumped into their seats.

Sports Bob joined Captain Slogg at the controls.

'Bob, they're trying to chew through the capsule's legs,' Slogg said. 'We need to get off the surface immediately.'

It was as much as Bob needed to know. He leapt into his seat with surprising agility and grabbed the controls.

Sports Bob threw on his earphones and talked rapidly with Mission Control.

Another shudder shook through the capsule, this one considerably more intense than the last.

'Belt yourselves in!' Captain Slogg called. 'We're going straight up.'

Sun Hee Wan strapped herself in next to Po Kwan. It wasn't ideal and she tried to give the injured man as much room as she could, but there were only three seats. Captain Slogg and Sports Bob were sharing one and that left Lee and Ho Chin to share the third. Well, at least Lee and Sun Hee Wan were small. They would manage.

After two further shudders the capsule's engines kicked in.

'Here goes!' Captain Slogg warned everyone.

The engines roared. The capsule strained. But it didn't lift-off.

'What's happening?' Lee asked.

'I ... don't know,' Sports Bob told him. 'I'm giving it normal thrust.'

'Give it a bit more, we're heavier than before, remember. Three extra passengers.'

The capsule shuddered again. For a fraction of a second it felt as if they were lifting off the ground, but then they seemed to stop.

'It's still not working,' Slogg said.

'I know, I know,' Sports Bob muttered, fiddling with dials.

Captain Slogg leaned forward and changed the view on the display so that it looked directly below them instead of across the surface. 'They're swarming all over the legs! That's why we can't move.'

Lee didn't understand at first. 'But I ... I thought we left the base behind when we took off. I thought that was what all lunar capsules did.'

'Used to,' the Captain told him. 'Not on this model though. The base is fixed to the capsule. It can't come off.'

While Captain Slogg explained all this to Lee, Sports Bob tried again, increasing the power. Slowly – painfully slowly – the capsule rose, edging them off the lunar surface. It felt like a millimetre each second, like a man pulling a train with his teeth.

'Have we thrown them off yet?' Sports Bob asked the captain, who leaned forward again. Leaning forward was not easy with Sports Bob sat next to him. Plenty of wriggling was required. But he managed.

As he did so, The Tin Can lurched to one side. 'Woah!' everyone cried.

'What's that?' Lee called to the captain.

'We've got them off one leg,' Slogg told them. 'Come on Bob!'

'I can't give it any more. There's nothing more to give!'

Lee had an idea.

'Drop the power suddenly, then kick it back in,' he suggested, remembering how he had avoided the Moon rat torpedo.

Captain Slogg agreed. 'It's worth a try.'

'Okay,' Sports Bob said. 'Prepare to feel ill.'

And two seconds later Lee found out exactly why Sports Bob had warned them. His stomach lurched as the capsule swung horribly, the pull of the Moon rats dragging them back towards the ground. He felt as if they were going to tilt right over and crash back to the surface.

And then a moment later the capsule hauled itself up again, like a boxer rising from the canvas after being knocked down. It was a strain to break away, but this time it was able to build up a bit more speed.

'Here goes!' Sports Bob called, and he pulled the lever back as far as it would go.

It was like trying to tear a telephone directory: hard to start but less difficult after the first few centimetres; as much about technique as about brute force.

Just as the Moon rats' combined resistance reached its maximum there was the sound of metal scraping against metal, like a spoon on the bottom of a pan. It was torture on the ears.

'We're doing it!'

When the final release came it was almost as shocking as their original blast off from Earth. With the engines at full power they ripped off the last of the Moon rats and shot into space.

Lee imagined a line of Moon rats tumbling back to the lunar surface ... and hoped they would explode when they hit it.

Chapter
Twenty-One

The journey home felt twice as long as the journey to the Moon. That was partly because there was less space in which to move around with six of them squashed into a capsule designed for three.

After a while they were able to remove their helmets.

Immediately all three Erokeans called 'Thank you!' to Sports Bob.

And Sun Hee Wan leaned over and kissed Lee on both cheeks before he knew what was happening. 'Thank you, Me Lee,' she said, smiling.

Lee blushed. 'Eh, yeah, whatever,' he mumbled, imagining all his classmates, saying 'Lee's got a girlfriend, Lee's got a girlfriend.'

No, he didn't have a girlfriend. Although if he was to have one sometime he hoped she would be like Sun Hee Wan.

It was a full twenty-four hours before they were able to say they were closer to Earth than to the Moon. By then they had redocked with the command module, which at least meant they had more leg room, even if it still didn't give them a seat each. They had also cast off the lunar module that had taken them to and from the surface. Lee was sad to see it float off into space. He wouldn't have minded quite so much if the Moon rat had still been in it, but Sports Bob had insisted on bringing it with him, albeit in another locked cupboard.

Passing halfway felt like progress and Lee's spirits rose. He thought about being back with his family. He hadn't missed them too much since he had blasted off because there had been so much to do, but he was homesick now that he was going to see them again soon, even though that seemed to make no sense.

However, as Lee was dreaming of dinner with his mum, dad and Rebecca – even if dinner was one of his mum's usual burnt offerings - Captain Slogg reminded him that they weren't home and dry yet.

'We'll be hitting Earth's atmosphere in about an hour,' the captain warned. 'Be ready for it. We'll get thrown around a good bit. And it will become very warm, even with all the tiles to deflect the heat. So helmets on in five minutes.'

'How long will we be thrown about for?'

'Not too long, I hope, but if you're planning a trip to the toilet it would be worth going before we hit the danger zone.'

'The "danger zone"?' Lee quizzed.

'I won't lie,' the captain said, 'it is dangerous. High

temperatures and high speeds ... not the ideal combination. But we'll be fine, I'm sure. I've never had a problem with it before.'

'Aw,' Lee said, thinking: *there's a first time for everything!*

And it was an entirely reasonable thought, because exactly thirty minutes later the capsule was clobbered by a giant bowling ball.

At least that was how it felt. The capsule was sent flying. Sparks flew up in front of the window and Sports Bob fought with the steering.

'Hold on, everyone!' the captain commanded.

It was the first time Lee or any of the Erokeans had experienced this sort of storm, and it was scary.

'Is it always like this?' Lee shouted.

'This is particularly bad,' came Sports Bob's reply into his helmet, which wasn't exactly reassuring. 'But we'll be through it soon enough.'

Five minutes ago wouldn't be too soon, Lee thought.

Down they plunged, through the layer of gases protecting Earth from stray objects floating around the solar system.

Po Kwan winced with every shudder. He was not enjoying being bashed around. His broken ribs were screaming 'STOP!' Lee wished he could help in some way, but there was nothing he could do other than nod his head to try to reassure Po Kwan that the jolting would soon stop and it would all be over.

Then The Tin Can took its strongest hit. Lee could have sworn that the capsule jumped a mile to the right and another mile downwards. His stomach certainly travelled that far and back again. He thought he was going to be sick. In fact he was sure he was going to be. Absolutely, definitely, completely and utterly certain he was going to be. He reached down the back of the captain's seat for a sick bag but there wasn't one there. And then he remembered that a sick bag would be no use anyway, he had a helmet on. Panic set in, as did visions of vomit sloshing about his visor. The smell would be unbearable.

Then as suddenly as the shaking had started it ceased and they were gliding back to Earth like a bird. It wasn't too long afterwards that Captain Slogg informed them they would be splashing down shortly.

Chapter
Twenty-Two

When they finally hit the water, three huge parachutes collapsing above them, it was Lee who was first to cry, 'We made it!'

'Thank you, thank you,' cried the Erokeans. 'Thank you, Me Lee.'

Captain Slogg nodded, relieved to have returned both crews to Earth in one piece.

Oh it was good to be back on the blue planet and to know that they would shortly be whisked aboard a comfortable ship.

While they waited, Lee flicked open the cupboard the Moon rat was in to check it was still dead. He was relieved to find that it apparently was. Sports Bob had talked during the return journey about keeping it as a pet if it could be trained to behave better than it had on the Moon. As far as Lee was concerned, he was welcome to it.

While the landing had been gentle the sea was rough. Waves tossed them up and down and from side to side. It wasn't doing Lee's stomach any favours again. He'd never been good on boats. He remembered being on a ferry once and having to lie down for half the journey.

Chapter Twenty-Two

Lying down wasn't an option in the capsule, it wasn't big enough. Plus he'd probably injure himself being thrown about. But he had to do *something* because once again he really was beginning to feel nauseous.

At least this time he didn't have his helmet on. Though that did present a danger to everyone else in the capsule. The danger of him spraying them all.

Under his breath he urged the recovery crew to hurry up. Where were they? What was holding them up? Because all the time he was growing worse.

And then the moment came when he knew it was going to happen, there was no stopping it.

And at that point instinct took over. He leaned back and stretched until his hand reached his helmet, which was hanging on the wall. He flicked the clip to release it and rapidly swung it down into his lap, narrowly missing Po Kwan's arm in doing so.

Two seconds later his head was over the helmet and he heaved straight into it.

So when the knock on the door came a few moments later it could not have been more welcome. And when, after some fiddling, Captain Slogg opened the hatch Lee sucked in the pure Earth air that rushed to greet him. It was better than any smiling dignitary. It had never occurred to him that air had either a taste or a smell, but, having grown used to what they had breathed on the Moon, followed by the stench from Lee's helmet of spew, his first breath tasted wonderful. Better than hot chocolate and a lot less fattening. It reminded him of home.

'Oi! Stop hogging the fresh stuff.' Sports Bob called to him. 'We all need some!'

Chapter
Twenty-Three

It's amazing how quickly classmates (and little sisters and school teachers) can forget that you're famous. Even if you've become the first kid ever to go to the Moon, they're impressed for five minutes and ask you loads of questions about it, but then someone brings in a football signed by their favourite player and your classmates focus their attention on that instead. One day a space hero, the next a boy who went somewhere unusual for his summer holidays. Somewhere further than most other pupils ... but where was it again?

Perhaps this should have bothered Lee. Perhaps he should have stood up in class once in a while and shouted, 'I've flown to the Moon and back! None of you have!' very loudly to remind everyone. But he didn't. He didn't because whether others thought what he had done was important didn't matter to him. *He* was proud of what he had achieved and that was all that mattered.

Reflecting on his adventure, Lee realised he had learned a huge amount: that listening was important; that he could still be a key part of a team even if everyone knew a lot more than him; that size isn't everything and that being smaller than others can have its advantages (it can sometimes save lives); and of course he had learned how to pee in space. Okay, he would probably never need to use that last piece of knowledge again, but who could say? He had no more idea what life held in store for him than did the next person.

And although some people didn't read the news headlines and so quickly forgot about Lee's exploits, two very important people didn't: his mum and dad. They were bursting with pride. One tiny bit more and they would explode with it, and what a mess that would make. It's good when you make your parents proud of you. It's not quite so good when you cause them to explode.

And all the citizens of a small country called Erokea also remembered what Lee had done for three of their number. There weren't many people in Erokea compared to most countries, but there were still a few million. And they were extremely grateful that Lee had risked his own life, not once but three times, to cross the Moon and rescue their stranded astronauts. It wasn't the sort of thing that happened every day.

Lee received an official letter from the Erokean ambassador inviting him and his family to travel to Erokea any time he wanted for a free holiday. It began:

Chapter Twenty-Three

Dear Mr Me Lee ...

It was tempting ... or it was until Lee checked the internet and found out what sort of dictator was running Erokea. Then he changed his mind. It seemed that visitors had a nasty habit of going missing in Erokea.

That said, something good did come from Lee's efforts. The Erokeans had to have some contact with the rest of the world in order to get their astronauts back. And talking is nearly always a good thing because it's only by speaking to people that you get to find out something about them. And once you know something about them you're normally inclined to show them a bit more respect. Perhaps the Erokean people wouldn't think everyone had it in for them after this episode ... even if their ruler still did.

More importantly, the post brought a letter from Po Kwan saying that he was recovering well from his broken ribs and other injuries. This meant much more to Lee. Po Kwan had been in terrible pain by the time they splashed down and was whisked off straight to hospital as soon as the doors were opened. So it was good to know that he was on the mend.

Oh, and you probably want to know about those Moon rats that caused Lee and the others so much trouble. What were they? Where did they come from?

Well, many years before they had been sent to the Moon at the command of the ruler of a small country who thought that the whole world was against him (hmm, sound familiar ...?). He had decided it might be a good idea to move to the Moon one day and so had spent billions of his country's money to send a rocket to establish if it would be possible. The rocket was un*manned*, but it wasn't un*ratted*.

The first rat was programmed to create a second rat, and the second to create a third and so on, all using equipment and parts stored on that rocket. Of course the idea was that once they had built a rat colony they would develop rapidly, eventually using the natural resources of the Moon to build a city that the ruler could move to if ever there was trouble. And the chances had been a) that there *would* be trouble, and b) that *he* would be the cause of the trouble – he was that sort of guy.

The Moon rats had managed the first task and had built each other, but when they tried to build a city they realised two things: first, that the Moon didn't have any natural resources that they could easily get hold of; and second, that it was much easier to just dig a burrow and live there. So that's what they did. And there was nothing the ruler could do about it. (The maker of the rats sensibly fled the country for fear of being jailed.) And let's be honest, it was a mad plan in the first place, which explains why it was completely forgotten about by the dictator's son (the new, equally bonkers dictator) when he took over the country a few years later.

So Lee slipped back into his old pre-Moon life almost as if nothing had happened.

However, he was allowed to keep one white, shiny reminder of his amazing journey: his helmet.

Well can you imagine anyone else wanting to wear it after Lee was sick into it?

Epilogue

I t had been another busy day for Sports Bob, one interview after another. Everyone wanted him to describe how he had fought off the Moon rats and flown his fellow astronauts to safety. If he'd told the tale once he'd told it a hundred times now, yet interviewers kept asking him to repeat it. He imagined Neil Armstrong must similarly have been asked, 'How did it feel to know you were the first human to step onto the Moon?' thousands of times in his life.

Sports Bob didn't mind, however, because it was all fuelling the public's interest in space and he thought they ought to know more about it.

Still, he was tired now. So he sat on the sofa to watch some sport on his television. He had a lot of catching up to do, having recorded all the games played while he had been in space. He couldn't allow himself to fall behind his friends by not knowing all the results.

So with a glass of orange juice in one hand, a remote control in the other and a warm breeze blowing through his open patio door, he stretched his legs and placed his large feet on the unusual footstool that was easily his favourite piece of furniture in the house. It was unusual because it was metallic, with a cushion on top for padding. And because it was a Moon rat.

Bob loved using the Moon rat as a footstool. It was the centrepiece for his lounge, a feature all his friends could admire and comment on. After all, no-one else had one.

This evening he was catching up on football. There had been some big games played and he had three hours of highlights to enjoy. Fantastic. He pressed the PLAY button on the remote control and watched as the TV came to life.

Two commentators were talking about what might happen in the game. 'Yes, blah blah,' Sports Bob said, 'Get on with it.' He fast-forwarded to the start of the action.

As the referee's whistle blew to start the game Bob felt a twinge in his ankle but ignored it and lifted his juice to his lips … only to pour it up his nose and over his face when his foot twitched again.

'Too long in space,' he laughed to himself. 'Must be affecting my muscles.'

He grabbed a paper towel from the kitchen and wiped himself down, then returned to the lounge and collapsed onto the sofa again. Once more he lifted his feet to place them on the harmless, mechanised Moon rat, only this time they missed it and landed back on the floor.

'What?' Sports Bob asked, confused. He stared at his legs and then at the footstool. How had he missed it? Were his eyes failing?

He tried one more time. Only this time the moon rat shot across the room and out the patio door.

THE END

Your Thoughts

If you have any thoughts about this book, or if you simply want to complain about the jokes in it, please contact Keith via his website:

www.keithcharters.co.uk

where you can also get details on more books in the Lee series.

It's not every day that a part of your body explodes, but Lee's appendix does exactly that, landing him in hospital.

Soon after his operation, Lee is shocked to discover that evil Consul Mutants are trying to take over the world. Worse still, the hospital he is stuck in contains the portal they are using to invade Earth.

Other kids might quake in their boots at this news, but not Lee. He's determined to save the planet and comes up with a cunning plan to stop the aliens.

This is the story of a fearless boy battling against intergalactic odds for the sake of mankind. Lee's only weapon is his intelligence ... which is a pity.

Lee and the Consul Mutants
Keith Charters
ISBN 978-1-905537-24-2
(paperback, RRP £6.99)

Meeting his dad's multizillionaire boss inspires Lee to come up with a get-rich-quick scheme of his own.

But not everyone is keen for Lee to succeed. Local shopkeeper Panface isn't, and it seems that he has sneaky spies out there, trying to ruin Lee's plans.

Will Lee get the better of his rivals? Or will he spend the whole time daydreaming about how many houses he'll own and how many butlers he'll have?

Lee will need to rely on his common sense and financial genius if he's to succeed in business ... so it could be a struggle.

Lee Goes For Gold
Keith Charters
ISBN 978-1-905537-25-9
(paperback, RRP £6.99)

Nothing is ever straightforward when Lee is around ... not even a summer holiday in Spain.

It ought to be a case of lazing by the pool, but Lee is soon spying on dodgy men in shiny suits and sunglasses, battling with a family that seems determined to ruin everyone's holiday and haranguing horrendous holiday reps.

With so much going on, how will Lee ever get a tan?

Lee's Holiday Showdown
Keith Charters
ISBN 978-1-905537-26-6
(paperback, RRP £6.99)

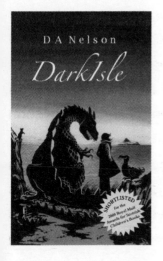

For 10-year-old Morag, there's nothing magical about the cellar of her cruel foster parents' home. But that's where she meets Aldiss, a talking rat, and his resourceful companion, Bertie the dodo. She jumps at the chance to run away and join them on their race against time to save their homeland from the evil warlock Devlish, who is intent on destroying it. But first, Bertie and Aldiss will need to stop bickering long enough to free the only guide who knows where to find Devlish: Shona, a dragon who's been turned to stone.

Together, these four friends begin their journey to a mysterious dark island beyond the horizon, where danger and glory await—along with clues to the disappearance of Morag's parents, whose destiny seems somehow linked to her own ...

DarkIsle
D A Nelson
ISBN 978-1-905537-04-4
(paperback, RRP £6.99)

The exciting sequel to the bestselling *DarkIsle*

Two months after she saved The Eye of Lornish, Morag is adjusting to life in the secret northern kingdom of Marnoch Mor. But dark dreams are troubling her and a spate of unexplained events prove that even with the protection of her friends—Shona the dragon, Bertie the dodo and Aldiss the rat—Morag is still not safe from harm ...

DarkIsle: Resurrection
D A Nelson
ISBN 978-1-905537-18-1
(paperback, RRP £6.99)

Twelve-year-old Bree McCready has a mission: she has just one night to save the world!

It starts when a clue inscribed on a Half-Heart Locket leads Bree and her best friends Sandy and Honey to an ancient magical book. With it they can freeze time, fly and shrink to the size of ants.

But they soon discover the book has a long history of destruction and death. And it's being sought by the monstrous Thalofedril, who will stop at nothing to get it.

Using its incredible powers, he could turn the world into a wasteland.

Bree, Sandy and Honey go on the run—hurtling off city rooftops, down neck-breaking ravines, and through night-black underground tunnels—to keep the book out of his lethal hands. Little do they know that the greatest danger of all lies ahead, in the heart of his deadly lair ...

Can Bree find the courage to face this terrifying evil, and to confront the secrets of her tragic past?

Bree McCready and the Half-Heart Locket
Hazel Allan
ISBN 978-1-905537-11-2
(paperback, RRP £6.99)

Everyone who came to the strange gym class was looking for something else. What they found was the mysterious Mrs Powell and Pashki, a lost art from an age when cats were worshipped as gods.

Ben and Tiffany wonder: who is their eccentric old teacher? What does she really want with them? And why are they suddenly able to see in the dark?

Meanwhile, in London's gloomy streets, human vermin are stirring. Ben and Tiffany may soon be glad of their new gifts. But against men whose cunning is matched only by their unspeakable cruelty, will even nine lives be enough?

The Cat Kin
Nick Green
ISBN 978-1-905537-16-7
(paperback, RRP £6.99)